The Daleks Invade Atlantis

Matthew Petchinsky

Apophis Enterprises LLC

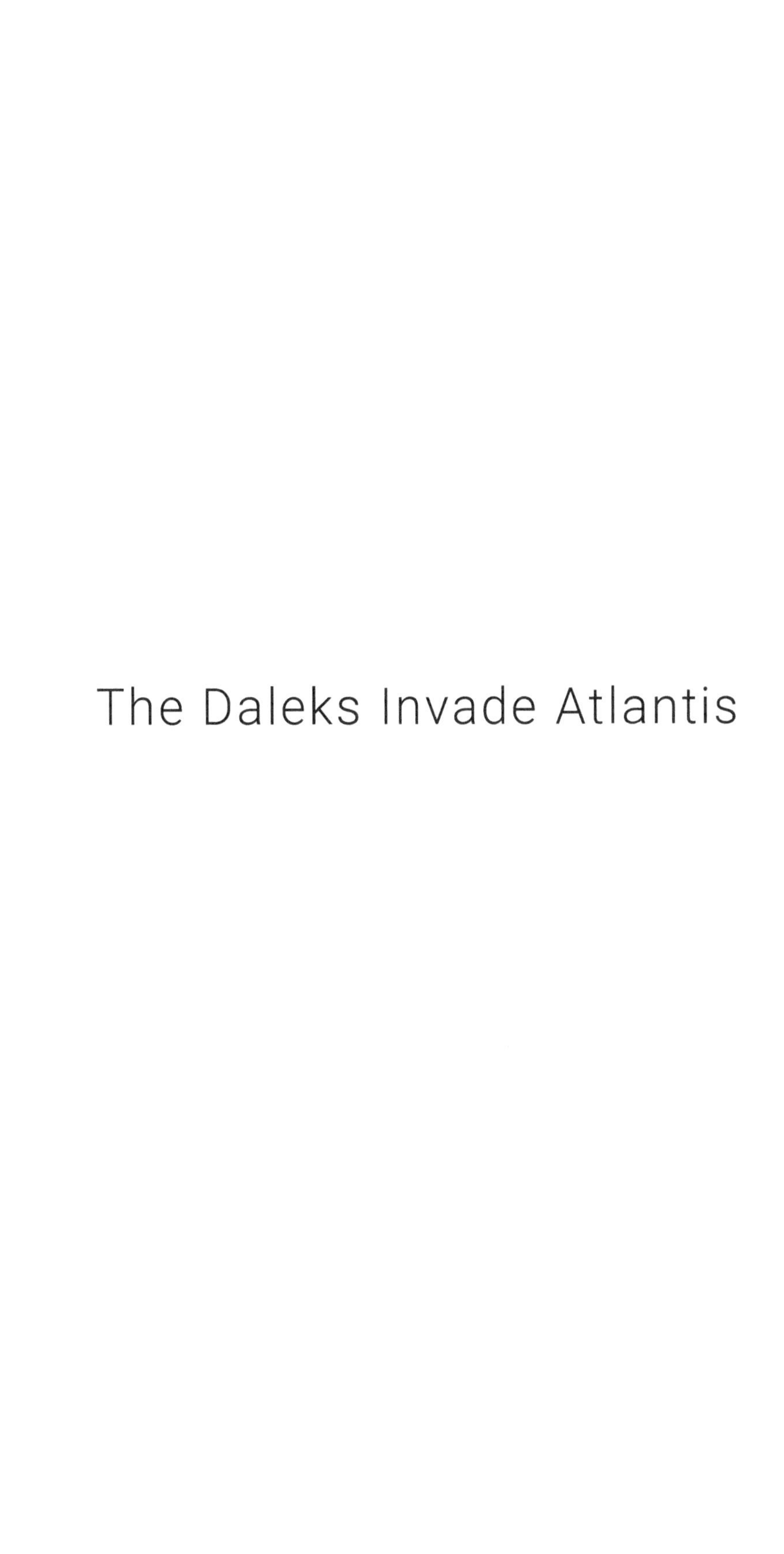
The Daleks Invade Atlantis

The Daleks Invade Atlantis

By: Matthew Petchinsky

-
-
-
-
-
-
-
-
-
-
-
-
-
-
-
-
-
-
-
-
-

-

-

-

-

-

<u>Disclaimer:</u>

This book is a fan-made story and is not officially affiliated with the creators or producers of "Doctor Who" or "Stargate Atlantis." All characters and original elements from "Doctor Who" and "Stargate Atlantis" remain the property of their respective rights holders. This story has been created purely for entertainment purposes and is not published for profit.

This work is intended to be a tribute to the original series, celebrating the characters and settings that fans love. No infringement of copyright is intended. The narrative and interpretations presented in this book are entirely the work of the author and represent a new, original contribution to the existing body of fan-made literature.

This story complies with legal guidelines for fan fiction and derivative works. The author has made every effort to ensure that all elements of the story that directly reference the original series are used in a manner consistent with fair use standards.

Chapter 1: Arrival in Atlantis

The hum of the TARDIS engines quieted, a sign they had materialized. Inside, the control room was aglow with the erratic dance of lights and dials that marked their unexpected arrival. The Third Doctor, with his flamboyant, flowing cape and white ruffled shirt, stood at the console, his fingers moving deftly over the controls. Beside him, Sarah Jane Smith, dressed in a practical jumper and jeans, looked around, puzzled.

"Doctor, where have we landed this time?" Sarah Jane asked, a mix of excitement and concern in her voice as she glanced at the unfamiliar readings on the console.

The Doctor, peering over his spectacles, chuckled softly. "Somewhere new, Sarah Jane! The readings are quite extraordinary. We're not just on another planet; we're inside another *kind* of ship. A city-ship, to be exact. Fascinating, isn't it?"

Before Sarah Jane could reply, the door of the TARDIS creaked open, revealing a sprawling room filled with futuristic technology and panels of blinking lights. They stepped out into a large, circular chamber dominated by a massive ring-like structure—the blue Atlantean Stargate. It stood inert but impressive, framed by towering metallic spires and illuminated pathways.

As they ventured further, their arrival didn't go unnoticed. From a corridor emerged Dr. Elizabeth Weir, the leader of the Atlantis expedition. She was a woman of poise, dressed in a standard off-world uniform, her face marked by both authority and curiosity. Behind her, a few members of her team peeked, equally stunned to see newcomers emerge from what appeared to be thin air.

"Hello there!" the Doctor greeted cheerfully, tipping his hat. "I'm the Doctor, and this is Sarah Jane Smith. And you are?"

Dr. Weir stepped forward, her initial shock giving way to diplomatic calm. "Dr. Elizabeth Weir. Welcome to Atlantis. But I must ask—how did you get here, and what exactly is *that*?" She gestured towards the TARDIS, her eyes narrowing slightly.

"Oh, the TARDIS? Time and Relative Dimension in Space," the Doctor explained with a wave of his hand. "A time machine, and so much more. We travel through time and space. And it seems we've landed in your...oh, what did you call it? Atlantis! Splendid!"

Sarah Jane stepped forward, offering a friendly smile. "We didn't mean to intrude. It's all a bit of an accident, really. The TARDIS has a mind of its own sometimes."

"We understand the concept of unexpected arrivals," Dr. Weir said, regaining her composure. "You're inside one of the most advanced pieces of technology created by the Ancients—Atlantis. This city is not just a ship; it's a legacy of a civilization long gone. You're standing in the control room, and that," she pointed to the Stargate, "is a Stargate, part of a network that spans galaxies."

The Doctor's eyes lit up with the thrill of discovery. "Oh, I do love a good network! Galaxies you say? Remarkable! And that gate, the blue hue is quite distinct from the ones I've seen. Does it function differently?"

"As far as we know, it functions the same as any other Stargate, just unique in design. It connects us to other worlds," Dr. Weir explained, moving towards the Stargate, inviting them to follow. "We use it to explore, to make alliances, to defend ourselves."

"Fascinating," the Doctor mused, walking around the Stargate, his fingers brushing against the cool, metallic surface. "And you, Elizabeth, are the caretaker of this marvelous place?"

Dr. Weir nodded. "I am. Along with my team, we try to unlock the secrets of the Ancients, maintain their technologies, and use them responsibly."

"Well, it seems we have much to discuss and perhaps assist each other in our mutual pursuits of knowledge," the Doctor said, beaming.

Sarah Jane laughed lightly. "We always seem to find ourselves in the middle of adventure, don't we, Doctor?"

"Indeed, Sarah Jane," the Doctor agreed, his eyes twinkling with excitement. "Indeed, we do."

Chapter 2: First Contact

After the initial introductions in the control room, Dr. Elizabeth Weir signaled for the rest of her team to join them. As they assembled, the buzz of whispered speculation filled the air. The team ranged from scientists and engineers to military personnel, all integral to the Atlantis expedition.

Dr. Weir cleared her throat, addressing her team with a calm authority. "Everyone, I'd like you to meet our unexpected guests, the Doctor and Sarah Jane Smith. They've arrived in what appears to be a... well, a very unique vessel called the TARDIS."

The Doctor stepped forward with a flourish, his eyes twinkling behind his spectacles. "Ah, yes, quite unique indeed. But let's not dwell on that. We're here now, by accident, but delighted nonetheless to explore such a remarkable place as Atlantis."

Sarah Jane offered a warm smile to the gathering crowd. "It's a pleasure to meet you all. We've heard so much already!"

One figure pushed through the crowd, a man with an air of impatience tempered by undeniable curiosity. Dr. Rodney McKay, head scientist of the Atlantis expedition, approached with a skeptical look. "A time machine? Really? Because that sounds scientifically impossible."

The Doctor's smile widened. "Oh, Dr. McKay, I assure you, it's quite possible with the right understanding of temporal mechanics and quantum theory. But I suspect you have technologies and achievements here that would seem equally impossible to those not in the know."

Intrigued despite himself, McKay nodded begrudgingly. "Well, when you put it that way... Perhaps you could offer some insights on our unsolved conundrums."

"Delighted to, but first, perhaps a tour?" the Doctor suggested.

Dr. Weir agreed, leading the way. As they walked through the corridors of Atlantis, the city's blend of stone-like structures and advanced technology was on full display. Vast windows revealed views of the ocean surrounding them, a reminder of the city's placement on the ocean floor.

"Atlantis is powered by three Zero Point Modules, or ZPMs," Dr. Weir explained. "They harness vacuum energy, providing almost limitless power."

"Fascinating! Zero Point Energy is quite the elusive beast in many universes," the Doctor commented, examining a power conduit panel with interest.

They continued to a large laboratory where Dr. McKay was eager to show off his latest project. "This is the ARX-7," McKay began, pointing to a sleek, metallic device on the central table. "It's a prototype drone designed to enhance our defensive capabilities."

The Doctor leaned in, his eyes scanning the intricate design. "Impressive! Autonomous, I presume? And capable of adaptive tactical responses?"

"Exactly," McKay replied, a hint of pride in his voice. "It learns from each encounter, improving its strategies over time."

As they discussed the technical details, Sarah Jane wandered slightly apart, engaging with a young scientist named Dr. Miko Kusanagi, who was monitoring data from the Pegasus galaxy. "What's all this?" Sarah Jane asked, gesturing to the swirling galaxy images on the screen.

"We're tracking gate activations and space anomalies," Miko explained. "It helps us keep ahead of the Wraith."

"The Wraith?" Sarah Jane echoed, intrigued.

"Yes, they are the primary threat in this galaxy—predatory creatures that feed on humans," Dr. Weir interjected, joining them. "It's why much of our technology is focused on defense and survival."

As the tour concluded, the group returned to the main control room, where the towering image of the Stargate remained a prominent feature. "We use the Stargate not just for exploration, but also to forge alliances and occasionally, to fight," Dr. Weir stated, her tone mixing pride with a hint of solemnity.

The Doctor, looking thoughtful, nodded slowly. "Incredible as this all is, Elizabeth, it's clear you bear a heavy responsibility."

"Yes," she agreed, "but one we carry with great honor."

"Indeed," the Doctor murmured. "And perhaps, with our accidental arrival, we can offer some assistance, especially with your scientific... conundrums?"

McKay, initially skeptical, now seemed genuinely interested. "Well, Doctor, if you're as brilliant as you claim, perhaps there's a thing or two we could learn from each other."

The Doctor's grin was all the answer McKay needed. They were, after all, scientists and explorers at heart, united by a common curiosity and a shared sky full of stars.

Chapter 3: Unsettling Discoveries

After the tour and discussions of scientific achievements, the group split up to pursue their respective interests within Atlantis. The Doctor, ever curious, wandered through the corridors with his sonic screwdriver in hand, scanning various technologies and architectural marvels. It wasn't long before his device beeped rapidly, indicating an anomaly.

"Ah, now what have we here?" the Doctor muttered to himself, examining the readouts with a furrowed brow. The readings were off the charts, not matching any typical energy signatures known to Atlantis.

Noticing his preoccupation, Major John Sheppard approached, his P-90 slung casually over his shoulder. "Something wrong, Doctor?"

"Possibly, Major. There's an unusual energy signature here, quite out of place. It's not Ancient technology, nor does it match the usual Atlantis energy patterns," the Doctor explained, gesturing for Sheppard to follow. "Care to join me on a little investigation?"

"Lead the way," Sheppard replied, signaling to Teyla, who was discussing training routines with Ronon nearby. She nodded and quickly joined them, her keen sense sharpened by the prospect of a new threat.

Together, they traced the energy signature to a seldom-used section of the city. The corridors here were dimly lit, the air filled with the hum of dormant technology. As they approached a sealed door, the Doctor's sonic screwdriver came alive again, its whirring a sharp contrast to the silence.

Using the device, the Doctor unsealed the door, which slid open with a hiss. Inside, the room was filled with relics and artifacts— seemingly a storage space for objects found throughout the galaxy that hadn't yet been cataloged.

"What is all this?" Teyla asked, her eyes scanning the room.

"Leftovers of explorations and encounters. Could be anything in here," Sheppard remarked, picking up a strangely shaped metal artifact before setting it back down.

The Doctor, meanwhile, honed in on the source of the energy signature. Tucked behind a stack of Ancient devices was a large, metallic object that was distinctly out of place. As they approached, the outline became unmistakable—a Dalek casing, dormant yet ominous.

"Doctor, is that what I think it is?" Sheppard asked, his hand instinctively going to his weapon.

"Yes, Major, unfortunately, it is a Dalek," the Doctor confirmed gravely. "And it's here, in Atlantis, which is not good at all. Not good one bit."

Teyla, unfamiliar with the Dalek, looked between them, sensing the severity of their reactions. "What is a Dalek? And why does it bring such concern?"

The Doctor turned to her, his expression serious. "Daleks are merciless beings, Teyla. Encased in armor like this, they are among the universe's most dangerous creatures, bent on conquest and destruction. Their presence here is... alarming."

"But it's just a casing, right? Could it not be empty?" Sheppard asked, though his tone lacked conviction.

The Doctor knelt beside the casing, sonic screwdriver in hand, scanning intensively. "While I hope you're right, we must assume it's a scout or a beacon—possibly a sign of more to come. We need to figure out how it got here, and more importantly, if it was alone."

He stood up, facing both Sheppard and Teyla. "We need to alert Dr. Weir immediately and prepare for the possibility of a threat. Daleks are not to be underestimated."

As they hurried out of the room, the weight of potential danger settled over them. They moved quickly through the corridors, the dormant Dalek casing left behind, an ominous reminder of what might come.

Chapter 4: Dalek Threat Detected

Back in the main control room of Atlantis, the atmosphere was charged with urgency. The Doctor, Sheppard, and Teyla quickly relayed their discovery to Dr. Weir, who listened with growing concern.

"The presence of a Dalek casing is deeply troubling," Dr. Weir said, her voice steady despite the tension. "Rodney, can we enhance our sensors to detect if there are more of them or, worse, if they're active?"

Dr. Rodney McKay, already at a console, nodded vigorously. "I'm on it, Elizabeth. If there's anything out there with energy signatures even remotely similar to the one the Doctor's device picked up, we'll find it."

As McKay and his team adjusted the sensors, the Doctor paced back and forth, his mind racing with possibilities. Sarah Jane watched him, knowing his experience with the Daleks spelled serious trouble.

The console beeped insistently, and a technician called out, "Dr. Weir, we're picking up something. It's a fleet—massive energy readings, just outside the Pegasus galaxy."

Everyone's attention snapped to the main screen, which displayed the alarming image of a large fleet of Dalek saucers poised at the edge of the galaxy.

"It's as I feared," the Doctor said gravely. "A Dalek fleet, and it's on our doorstep. This is no coincidence—they're here for a reason."

Dr. Weir turned to him, her expression resolute. "Doctor, tell us everything you know. How can we prepare for this?"

Gathering the team around, the Doctor began, "Daleks are creatures of hate, encased in armor nearly impervious to most weaponry. They conquer and exterminate without remorse. Their technology is advanced, and their strategic capabilities are terrifyingly efficient."

Sheppard interjected, "What about their weaknesses? There has to be a way to stop them."

The Doctor nodded. "Indeed, Major. Daleks have vulnerabilities, though few. Their eyestalk is a primary sensory organ, and impairing it can blind them, albeit temporarily. Electromagnetic pulses can disrupt their systems. But the real challenge is reaching them—they're usually shielded, and their firepower is immense."

McKay spoke up, adjusting his glasses. "We have Ancient technology at our disposal—drones, shields, and the chair. Maybe we can adapt some of it to enhance our defenses against these... Daleks."

"We need to act swiftly," Dr. Weir decided. "Rodney, work with the Doctor to integrate whatever you can from our technology with his knowledge of the Daleks. John, Teyla, prepare everyone for a possible incursion. We need to be ready for anything."

As the team dispersed to their assignments, tension filled the room. Sarah Jane approached the Doctor, her concern evident. "Doctor, can we really stop them this time?"

"We must, Sarah Jane," the Doctor replied, his voice firm. "And we will. We have something here we didn't have in our previous encounters —Atlantis itself. Its mysteries and capabilities might just give us the edge we need."

Meanwhile, McKay and the Doctor huddled over a schematic of Atlantis' defense systems, plotting each move with precision. "If we reroute power from the non-essential systems, we could enhance the output of the drone weapons," McKay suggested.

"And if we modify the shield frequency to oscillate at a rate that disrupts Dalek sensors, we might just blind them as they approach," the Doctor added, his brain ticking through solutions.

The control room buzzed with activity, everyone moving with purpose. Despite the fear of the looming threat, there was a sense of unity and determination. Atlantis had faced many dangers before, but the Dalek fleet presented a new and horrifying challenge. Preparations accelerated as the alien ships drew nearer, the silent threat of extermination hanging over them all.

Chapter 5: Ancient Defenses

The control room of Atlantis was a flurry of activity as everyone prepared for the imminent arrival of the Dalek fleet. The Doctor, McKay, and Sheppard headed towards the Ancient drone chair room, their footsteps echoing through the corridors. Teyla followed closely, ready to assist in any way she could.

As they entered the chamber, the sight of the drone chair—a sleek, metallic seat surrounded by intricate controls and conduits—filled them with a mixture of hope and anxiety. This was Atlantis' primary line of defense, and its activation was crucial to their survival.

"Alright, McKay, let's get this thing up and running," Sheppard urged, his tone tense but focused.

McKay, already sweating, approached the chair and began typing commands into a nearby console. "I'm trying, but this Ancient technology is notoriously temperamental. One wrong move and we could disable half the city's systems instead of activating the drones."

The Doctor, standing beside him, examined the readouts with keen interest. "Ancient technology often requires a touch of finesse, Dr. McKay. Perhaps if we reconfigure the power conduits to direct more energy to the chair's interface?"

McKay frowned, his fingers flying over the controls. "Easy for you to say, Doctor. This is delicate work, and we don't have the luxury of time."

Suddenly, the room's lights flickered, and the console beeped with an error message. McKay cursed under his breath. "Damn it! The power grid is overloading. If I can't balance it, we could have a city-wide blackout."

The Doctor's eyes lit up with an idea. "Have you considered using a feedback loop? It could stabilize the energy flow."

"A feedback loop? That's insane! The feedback could cause a cascade failure," McKay snapped, his frustration evident.

"Or it could stabilize the system just enough to give us control," the Doctor countered, his voice calm but insistent. "We don't have many options, Rodney."

Sheppard, watching the exchange, weighed the risks. "Do it. We need those drones operational. McKay, trust the Doctor."

Reluctantly, McKay adjusted the settings, his hands shaking slightly. The Doctor assisted, his fingers deftly moving across the controls. As they initiated the feedback loop, the room's hum intensified, and the chair's interface lit up with a golden glow.

"It's working!" Teyla exclaimed, her relief palpable.

McKay breathed a sigh of relief. "For now. But we need to be careful. This system is on a knife's edge."

The Doctor took a seat in the drone chair, his expression determined. "Alright, let's see if we can give those Daleks a warm welcome."

As the Doctor activated the drones, the control room's screens displayed the drones emerging from hidden compartments throughout the city. They soared into the sky, forming a defensive perimeter around Atlantis.

"Incoming!" shouted a technician. "The Dalek fleet is within firing range."

Outside, the first wave of Dalek saucers approached, their metallic hulls gleaming ominously. The drones, now fully operational, fired streams of energy, striking several saucers and causing them to explode in brilliant flashes of light.

"Direct hits! We're taking them down!" Sheppard cheered, his eyes fixed on the screen.

But the celebration was short-lived. The Daleks, relentless and adaptive, began returning fire. Their powerful beams sliced through the air, striking several drones and sending them plummeting into the ocean below.

"Doctor, we're losing drones fast!" McKay yelled, panic rising in his voice.

The Doctor remained focused, adjusting the chair's controls. "We need to draw their fire away from the drones. If we can create a diversion, we might just buy ourselves enough time."

Suddenly, a massive explosion rocked the city. An energy beam from a Dalek saucer had struck one of the main towers, causing it to collapse in a shower of debris. Alarms blared, and the lights flickered ominously.

"Structural integrity compromised! We have casualties in the tower!" a technician reported, his voice strained with urgency.

"We can't take much more of this," Sheppard said, his face pale. "Doctor, what can we do?"

The Doctor's mind raced. "We need to disrupt their formation. If we can scatter their fleet, we can pick them off one by one."

"How?" McKay asked, desperation creeping into his tone.

"By creating a massive energy burst," the Doctor replied. "We can overload the ZPMs just enough to send out a pulse. It'll be risky, but it could work."

"That could blow us all to pieces!" McKay protested.

"Or it could save Atlantis," the Doctor countered. "We have to try."

Dr. Weir, who had been monitoring the situation from the control room, chimed in over the comms. "Do it, Doctor. We trust you."

The Doctor nodded and began the delicate process of overloading the ZPMs. McKay assisted, his initial skepticism giving way to a focused determination. As the energy levels surged, the city trembled, and sparks flew from the consoles.

"Ready... now!" the Doctor shouted, initiating the pulse.

A blinding flash of light erupted from Atlantis, spreading outwards and enveloping the Dalek fleet. The saucers were thrown into disarray, their formation shattered. Several Dalek ships collided, exploding in mid-air.

"We did it! We've disrupted their attack!" Teyla exclaimed, relief washing over her.

But the victory came at a cost. The overloaded systems began to fail, causing explosions and fires throughout the city. "We've got fires on multiple levels! Casualties reported!" a technician shouted.

"We need to stabilize the power grid before it's too late," McKay said, frantically working the controls.

The Doctor, exhausted but determined, continued his efforts. "Almost there... just a little more..."

As the fires raged and the Daleks regrouped for another attack, the fate of Atlantis hung in the balance. The team's resolve was tested to its limits, but they knew they had to hold on—for the city, for their survival, and for the hope of defeating the Daleks once and for all.

Chapter 6: Invasion Begins

The Dalek fleet, momentarily disrupted by the energy pulse, quickly reformed its ranks. The Atlantis team watched in horror as the saucers advanced with renewed determination, their ominous shapes growing larger on the main screen.

"They're coming!" shouted a technician. "Shields are failing!"

The Doctor's expression was grim. "Prepare for ground combat. Everyone, to your stations!"

The control room erupted into organized chaos as personnel grabbed weapons and donned protective gear. Major Sheppard took command, his voice calm but urgent. "Teams Alpha and Bravo, with me! We're defending the central spire. Everyone else, hold the control room at all costs!"

The Doctor, Sarah Jane, and McKay joined Dr. Weir at the command console, trying to coordinate the city's defenses. "Doctor, any last-minute tricks?" Dr. Weir asked, her voice strained with the weight of responsibility.

"We need to slow them down," the Doctor replied, his mind racing. "Divert power to the remaining drones and set them to intercept. And McKay, see if you can rig some of the inactive Stargates to emit an energy burst when they detect Dalek signatures."

"On it," McKay said, his fingers flying over the console.

Suddenly, the room shuddered violently. The first Dalek ship had breached the city's outer defenses, crashing into the lower levels. Explosions rocked Atlantis as the invaders poured through the breach.

"Daleks have entered the city!" a security officer reported. "They're advancing on multiple fronts!"

Sheppard led his team through the twisting corridors, the sounds of battle echoing around them. "Stay sharp, everyone. These things are ruthless."

They rounded a corner and came face to face with a squad of Daleks. "EX-TER-MINATE!" the Daleks chanted in unison, their weapons firing deadly beams.

"Take cover!" Sheppard shouted, diving behind a support pillar as beams of energy seared the air. His team returned fire, but the Daleks' shields absorbed most of the blasts.

"Flank them! Get behind their shields!" Sheppard ordered, signaling for two soldiers to move around the enemy. One soldier managed to get a clear shot, hitting a Dalek in its eyestalk. The Dalek screamed, "VISION IMPAIRED! VISION IMPAIRED!" before it exploded in a shower of sparks.

But the victory was short-lived. More Daleks surged forward, their weapons cutting down the soldiers who had flanked them. Sheppard fired relentlessly, his P-90 chattering, but it was clear they were being overwhelmed.

Back in the control room, the Doctor monitored the battle on the screens, his face tense. "We need to disrupt their command structure. If we can take out their leader, we might slow their advance."

"How do we find their leader?" Sarah Jane asked, her eyes wide with worry.

"Dalek commanders often remain on their ships, but with this much firepower, they'll be somewhere close," the Doctor replied. "We need to draw them out."

An explosion rocked the control room as a Dalek beam tore through the wall. "They're here!" McKay shouted, grabbing a pistol.

The first Dalek rolled into the room, its weapon swiveling to target the nearest human. "EX-TER-MINATE!" it screeched, firing a beam that narrowly missed Dr. Weir.

"Everyone, down!" the Doctor yelled, pulling Sarah Jane to the floor. He scrambled for his sonic screwdriver, using it to create a feedback loop in the Dalek's systems. The Dalek convulsed, sparks flying, and then exploded.

"We need to get to the lower levels," the Doctor said urgently. "If we can reach the main power conduit, we can set a trap."

Dr. Weir nodded. "Go! We'll hold them here as long as we can."

Sheppard and his team continued to fight fiercely, but the Daleks were relentless. One by one, his soldiers fell, their screams lost in the din of battle. Sheppard was thrown back by an explosion, his vision blurred as he struggled to rise.

"Major! We're getting overrun!" a soldier shouted before being hit by a Dalek beam.

Sheppard, bloodied but determined, fired his last rounds before his weapon clicked empty. He saw Teyla fighting valiantly, her combat skills pushing back a Dalek momentarily. But there were too many. He grabbed a fallen soldier's grenade, pulled the pin, and charged at the nearest Dalek.

"For Atlantis!" Sheppard yelled as he shoved the grenade into the Dalek's casing. The explosion took out the Dalek and sent Sheppard flying back, his body slamming into a wall. He lay still, unconscious or worse, amidst the wreckage.

The Doctor, Sarah Jane, and McKay reached the main power conduit, their path littered with debris and bodies. "We need to create an overload," the Doctor explained. "It will buy us time, but we have to be ready to evacuate."

"How much time do we have?" McKay asked, his hands trembling as he worked.

"Not enough," the Doctor replied grimly. "Sarah Jane, help me with these cables."

Together, they rigged the conduit to overload, the city's lights flickering as power surged through the system. The Doctor set the final connection, and a deep hum filled the air.

"That should do it. Now we need to get clear before it blows," the Doctor said, grabbing Sarah Jane's hand.

As they ran back towards the control room, the overloaded conduit exploded, sending shockwaves through the city. Daleks were thrown off balance, their advance momentarily halted.

In the control room, Dr. Weir and the remaining defenders braced for the impact. The ceiling cracked, and debris rained down as the explosion echoed through the halls.

"We can't hold them much longer!" a soldier shouted, firing his last rounds.

The Doctor and Sarah Jane burst into the room, out of breath but alive. "We need to evacuate now!" the Doctor yelled.

"There's nowhere to go," Dr. Weir replied, despair in her eyes. "We're surrounded."

"We'll find a way," the Doctor insisted. "We always do."

As the Daleks closed in, the team prepared for a final stand. The Doctor, his sonic screwdriver ready, faced the invaders with defiance. "This isn't over," he vowed, determination burning in his eyes.

But as the Daleks advanced relentlessly, the fate of Atlantis hung by a thread, and the cost of survival became ever more dire.

Chapter 7: Strategic Retreat

The aftermath of the explosion left Atlantis in a state of chaos. Fires burned unchecked, and the wail of alarms echoed through the corridors. The city's defenses were crumbling, and the relentless advance of the Daleks forced the team into a desperate retreat.

"We can't hold them here any longer," Dr. Weir said, her voice tight with urgency. "Fall back to the central control room. It's our best chance."

The remnants of the defense teams regrouped, carrying their wounded as they retreated. The corridors were filled with smoke and debris, and the sounds of battle grew ever closer. The Doctor, leading the way with Sarah Jane at his side, turned to Sheppard and Teyla.

"John, Teyla, we need to buy time. Get as many people as you can to the control room. I'll devise a plan to disrupt the Dalek operations from within."

Sheppard nodded, his face grim. "You heard him. Move out!"

As the team moved through the corridors, the Daleks' relentless pursuit was punctuated by bursts of laser fire and explosions. The Doctor and Sarah Jane worked frantically, using the sonic screwdriver to seal doors and create temporary barriers, but it was only a matter of time before the Daleks broke through.

"We're almost there," the Doctor urged, pushing a makeshift barricade into place.

When they finally reached the central control room, the team quickly reinforced the entrance with whatever they could find—tables, chairs, and debris piled high. Dr. Weir coordinated the efforts, her calm demeanor holding the group together.

"Doctor, we can't keep this up forever," she said, her eyes meeting his.

"I know," the Doctor replied, his mind racing. "But we don't have to. We just need enough time to turn the tide. I'm going to need access to the mainframe and any information you have on the Daleks' current operations."

McKay, despite his exhaustion, jumped into action, his fingers flying over the console. "Here, I've pulled up everything we've got. But Doctor, what exactly are you planning?"

The Doctor's eyes sparkled with a mix of determination and urgency. "A little sabotage. If we can disrupt their command network and disable their internal systems, we might just have a chance to push them back."

Teyla, listening intently, stepped forward. "What can we do to help?"

The Doctor looked at her and Sheppard. "Rally the remaining personnel. We need to organize a counter-offensive. Create as much chaos as possible to distract the Daleks while I work on disabling their systems."

Sheppard nodded, turning to his remaining team members. "Alright, you heard the Doctor. We're going to hit them hard and fast. Teyla, take a squad and secure the west wing. We need to keep them off balance."

Teyla, ever the warrior, nodded firmly. "We will do what we must."

The Doctor set to work at the console, interfacing with Atlantis' systems. McKay hovered nearby, ready to assist. "Doctor, if you over-load their central command module, it could create a feedback loop that would disable their entire network."

"Precisely what I was thinking," the Doctor replied, his hands moving swiftly. "But we need to be careful. One wrong move and we could take out our own systems instead."

As the Doctor worked, Sarah Jane moved through the room, offering words of encouragement to the beleaguered defenders. The tension was palpable, but her presence provided a small measure of comfort amidst the chaos.

Suddenly, the door to the control room shook violently, the sound of Dalek lasers and metallic voices echoing through the barrier. "EX-TER-MINATE!"

"We're running out of time," Sheppard warned, readying his weapon.

"Just a few more moments," the Doctor muttered, sweat beading on his forehead. "McKay, reroute the power through the auxiliary conduits."

"Got it," McKay replied, his hands flying over the controls. "Power rerouted."

The Doctor made a final adjustment and then slammed his hand down on the console. "Now!"

A surge of energy rippled through the system, and the screens flickered. For a moment, everything went dark, and then the room was filled with the sound of distorted Dalek voices.

"Systems malfunction! Systems malfunction!"

"It's working!" Sarah Jane exclaimed, her face lighting up with hope.

But the victory was short-lived. The door to the control room exploded inward, and Daleks began to pour through the breach. "EX-TER-MINATE!" they chanted, their weapons firing.

Sheppard and his team opened fire, a fierce battle erupting in the confined space. Teyla, leading her squad, fought with a combination of gunfire and hand-to-hand combat, her movements fluid and deadly.

The Doctor, still at the console, continued to disrupt the Dalek systems, each keystroke sending more chaos into their ranks. "Just a little longer," he whispered to himself.

Amidst the battle, a Dalek's laser struck a young soldier, who fell with a cry. Dr. Weir, despite the danger, rushed to his side, trying to drag him to safety. Another explosion rocked the room, sending debris flying and knocking several defenders to the ground.

"Doctor, we can't hold them much longer!" Sheppard yelled, his voice barely audible over the din of battle.

"Almost there," the Doctor replied, his fingers moving with desperate speed.

A Dalek targeted Sheppard, its weapon charging. At the last moment, Teyla threw herself in front of him, her P-90 firing. The Dalek exploded, but Teyla was thrown back by the blast, hitting the wall hard.

"Teyla!" Sheppard shouted, rushing to her side.

"I'm... alright," Teyla gasped, though her face was pale with pain.

Finally, the Doctor hit the last command, and the Daleks' systems went into full meltdown. "Now!" he shouted. "Push them back!"

With renewed vigor, the defenders surged forward. The Daleks, their systems failing, were less coordinated and easier targets. Sheppard and his team drove them back step by step, regaining control of the room.

"We did it," McKay said, his voice a mix of relief and disbelief. "We actually did it."

But the cost was high. The room was filled with the wounded and the dead, and the city's defenses were in tatters. The Doctor, his face grim, turned to Dr. Weir. "This is far from over. The Daleks will regroup. We need to be ready."

Dr. Weir nodded, her expression resolute despite the devastation around them. "We will be. We have to be."

As the team began to regroup and tend to the wounded, the Doctor looked out at the shattered city. The battle was won, but the war was far from over. And in the silence that followed, the promise of more bloodshed loomed heavy over Atlantis.

Chapter 8: Sabotage Mission

The temporary victory in the control room had given the team a brief respite, but the looming threat of the Daleks regrouping hung over Atlantis like a dark cloud. The Doctor knew they needed to act quickly to prevent the Daleks from regaining their full strength. Gathering Sarah Jane and Dr. Rodney McKay, he outlined their next move.

"We need to hit them where it hurts," the Doctor explained. "If we can disrupt their communications, we'll create chaos in their ranks. It'll buy us the time we need to fortify our defenses."

McKay, still skeptical but willing to follow the Doctor's lead, nodded. "Alright, but how do we get past their patrols? The city's crawling with Daleks."

The Doctor smiled, a glint of mischief in his eyes. "We use their arrogance against them. Daleks believe they are the supreme beings of the universe. They won't expect a small, determined team to infiltrate their occupied zones."

Sarah Jane, always ready for action, added, "And we use our knowledge of the city to our advantage. Rodney, you know the layout better than anyone."

McKay sighed, running a hand through his hair. "Alright, let's do this. But if we get caught, we're all dead."

The trio set out, navigating through the labyrinthine corridors of Atlantis. The once-bustling halls were now eerily silent, punctuated only by the distant hum of Dalek machinery and the occasional sound of gunfire from scattered skirmishes.

As they approached the first Dalek-occupied area, the Doctor held up a hand, signaling for silence. "We'll need to move quickly and quietly. McKay, how close are we to the main communication hub?"

McKay checked his handheld scanner, his eyes darting over the readings. "About 300 meters that way," he whispered, pointing down a dimly lit corridor.

They crept forward, their senses on high alert. As they rounded a corner, they saw a patrol of three Daleks scanning the area with their eyestalks. The Doctor motioned for them to hide behind a large support pillar, holding his breath as the Daleks passed by, their metallic voices echoing in the confined space.

"EX-TER-MINATE any intruders," one of the Daleks commanded, its voice cold and mechanical.

Once the Daleks were out of earshot, the Doctor turned to Sarah Jane and McKay. "We need to plant the first device here. It'll create a feedback loop in their communication systems."

Sarah Jane pulled out a small, cylindrical device from her bag and handed it to the Doctor. "Got it. Where do you need it?"

The Doctor pointed to a control panel embedded in the wall. "Right there. It needs to interface with their power supply."

McKay, ever the perfectionist, took the device from Sarah Jane. "Let me. If this goes wrong, we might alert every Dalek in the city."

He carefully opened the panel and connected the device, his hands steady despite the pressure. "Alright, it's in place. Now what?"

The Doctor activated the device with his sonic screwdriver, a faint hum indicating it was working. "That's one down. We need to place three more to cover all their communication relays."

They moved on, encountering more Dalek patrols along the way. At one point, they had to duck into a storage room to avoid detection. Inside, Sarah Jane spotted an old, discarded piece of Ancient technology.

"Doctor, look at this," she whispered, holding up the device.

The Doctor examined it, a smile spreading across his face. "A portable cloaking field! This could come in handy."

Using the cloaking device, they managed to bypass several more Dalek patrols, moving swiftly through the city. At the second location, they encountered their first real resistance. A group of Daleks guarded the relay station, their eyestalks scanning methodically.

"We can't get close enough to plant the device," McKay whispered, frustration evident in his voice.

Sarah Jane, always resourceful, had an idea. "Leave it to me." She pulled a small mirror from her bag and used it to reflect a beam of light down the corridor, creating a distraction.

The Daleks, their sensors detecting the movement, moved away from the relay station to investigate. "What is this? IN-TRUDER DE-TEC-TED!" one of them shouted.

"Now!" Sarah Jane hissed, and the Doctor and McKay rushed forward, planting the second device.

As they activated it, the Daleks realized they had been tricked and started to return. "MOVE!" the Doctor shouted, and they sprinted down the corridor, the sound of Dalek blasters firing behind them.

They narrowly escaped, ducking into a maintenance shaft. McKay, panting heavily, looked at Sarah Jane with a newfound respect. "That was... impressive. You saved our skins back there."

Sarah Jane smiled, a twinkle in her eye. "Just doing my part."

With two devices in place, they pressed on to the third location. The tension was palpable as they moved through the darkened corridors, every shadow a potential threat. The third relay station was in a more open area, heavily guarded by Daleks.

"We'll need a bigger distraction this time," the Doctor mused, looking around.

Sarah Jane's eyes fell on a control panel labeled "Emergency Ventilation System." "What about this? If we overload it, it might cause a system-wide alert."

McKay nodded, his face lighting up. "That could work. It'll draw them away from the relay station."

While McKay worked on overloading the ventilation system, the Doctor and Sarah Jane positioned themselves near the relay station. As the ventilation system went into overdrive, alarms blared throughout the area.

"ALERT! ALERT! MALFUNCTION DETECTED!" the Daleks chanted, moving towards the source of the disturbance.

With the Daleks distracted, the Doctor and Sarah Jane quickly planted the third device. As they activated it, the lights flickered, and the sound of Dalek communications began to distort.

"That's three. One more to go," the Doctor said, urgency in his voice.

The final relay station was deep within the Dalek-occupied zone, and the path to it was fraught with danger. They moved carefully, using the cloaking device to avoid detection. At one point, they had to crawl through a narrow maintenance tunnel, their progress slow and arduous.

When they finally reached the fourth relay station, they found it heavily fortified. Dalek sentries were posted at every entrance, their weapons at the ready.

"We'll never get past them," McKay said, despair creeping into his voice.

"We have to," the Doctor replied, determination in his eyes. "This is our only chance."

Sarah Jane, ever resourceful, had one last idea. "What if we use the cloaking device to create a decoy? We can make it seem like we're attacking from the other side."

The Doctor nodded, impressed by her quick thinking. "Brilliant! Let's do it."

They set up the cloaking device to emit a series of false signals, drawing the Daleks away from their positions. As the Daleks moved to intercept the imaginary threat, the trio rushed forward and planted the final device.

The Doctor activated it, and the entire Dalek communication network went haywire. "We did it! Now, let's get out of here!"

As they made their way back to the control room, the city echoed with the sounds of Dalek confusion and chaos. "COMMUNICA-TIONS FAILING! SYSTEMS MALFUNCTION!"

Back in the control room, the team watched on the screens as the Daleks floundered, their attacks becoming disorganized and ineffective.

"We've done it," Dr. Weir said, relief evident in her voice. "We've bought ourselves some time."

The Doctor, exhausted but triumphant, turned to Sarah Jane and McKay. "You both were incredible. We couldn't have done it without you."

McKay, his skepticism finally gone, nodded. "Yeah, well... maybe you're not so bad after all, Doctor."

Sarah Jane smiled, her heart swelling with pride. "Just another day saving the universe."

As the team regrouped and prepared for the next phase of their defense, they knew the battle was far from over. But for the first time, there was a glimmer of hope. The Daleks had been dealt a serious blow, and with the Doctor's help, they were ready to continue the fight for Atlantis.

Chapter 9: Dalek Counterattack

The temporary success of the sabotage mission had bought the Atlantis team some time, but it was clear that the Daleks would not be deterred for long. Back in the central control room, the atmosphere was tense. The team braced for the inevitable retaliation from the Daleks, knowing that their next move could very well decide the fate of Atlantis.

"They're regrouping," McKay reported, his eyes glued to the surveillance screens. "Their communications are still disrupted, but they're adapting quickly. We don't have much time."

The Doctor, pacing back and forth, stopped suddenly. "We need to get the Ancient drone chair back online. It's our best chance of mounting a strong defense."

"McKay, can you and the Doctor get it working again?" Dr. Weir asked, her voice tight with urgency.

McKay nodded. "We'll do our best. Just keep those Daleks out of here as long as you can."

Suddenly, the control room shook violently as an explosion tore through one of the outer walls. Debris rained down, and the team was thrown off their feet. "They're here!" a soldier shouted, scrambling to his feet and grabbing his weapon.

Daleks burst through the breach, their metallic voices echoing ominously. "EX-TER-MINATE! EX-TER-MINATE!"

"Fall back and hold the line!" Sheppard ordered, firing his P-90 at the advancing Daleks. Energy beams lanced through the air, striking the Daleks' shields with little effect.

Teyla, wielding a combination of an Atlantean energy weapon and her combat skills, took down a Dalek that had broken through the front lines. Her swift movements and precise strikes were a testament to her warrior heritage.

As the battle raged, the Doctor and McKay made their way to the drone chair room, navigating through the chaos. They had to duck and dodge as explosions rocked the city and debris flew in all directions.

"We're almost there!" the Doctor shouted over the din. "Just a little further!"

They finally reached the drone chair room, but it was already under attack. Several Daleks were firing at the entrance, trying to breach the defenses. "We need to clear them out!" McKay yelled, grabbing a nearby energy rifle and firing at the Daleks.

The Doctor joined in, using his sonic screwdriver to disable the Daleks' shields momentarily. "Now, McKay! Hit them hard!"

McKay fired a concentrated burst, taking down two Daleks. The remaining Daleks turned their attention to the new threat, their weapons charging. "IN-TRU-DERS WILL BE EX-TER-MIN-ATED!"

Before they could fire, a blast from behind destroyed the Daleks, scattering their remains across the room. Sheppard and Teyla had arrived, providing much-needed backup. "We thought you might need some help," Sheppard said, a grim smile on his face.

"Perfect timing," the Doctor replied. "Let's get this chair operational."

As McKay worked on the chair's controls, the Doctor interfaced with the Ancient systems, trying to reroute power and bypass damaged circuits. "Come on, come on," the Doctor muttered, his hands moving rapidly.

In the control room, the battle intensified. Daleks swarmed through the breach, their weapons cutting down defenders left and right. Dr. Weir, coordinating the defense, knew they were running out of time and resources. "Hold the line! Don't let them through!" she shouted, firing her pistol at an approaching Dalek.

A soldier next to her was hit by a Dalek beam, falling to the ground with a cry. Dr. Weir dragged him to cover, her heart pounding with fear and determination. "Stay with me," she urged, pressing a cloth to his wound.

The Daleks advanced relentlessly, their mechanical voices chanting "EX-TER-MIN-ATE!" with every step. The defenders were pushed back, their numbers dwindling as the Daleks pressed forward.

Back in the drone chair room, McKay finally managed to stabilize the power grid. "It's ready!" he shouted, wiping sweat from his brow.

The Doctor took his place in the chair, activating the drones. The room filled with a golden glow as the drones powered up and launched into the air. "Let's see how you like this!" the Doctor declared, directing the drones towards the Daleks.

In the control room, the drones swooped in, their energy beams striking the Daleks with deadly precision. Several Daleks were destroyed in quick succession, their metallic shells exploding in showers of sparks.

"We're pushing them back!" Sheppard shouted, rallying his team. "Keep firing!"

Teyla fought with renewed vigor, her movements a blur of deadly efficiency. She took down another Dalek, but a stray beam caught her in the shoulder, sending her sprawling to the ground. Sheppard rushed to her side, pulling her to safety. "Hang in there, Teyla. We've got this."

Despite their best efforts, the Daleks continued to advance. The drones, though effective, were not enough to stem the tide. The defenders were pushed back to the central control room, making a final stand against the overwhelming force.

Dr. Weir, her face grim, knew they had only one option left. "Doctor, we need to evacuate the city. If we can't hold them here, we need to save as many lives as possible."

The Doctor, his face set with determination, nodded. "I understand. McKay, initiate the evacuation protocols. We need to get everyone to the Jumper Bay."

As McKay worked to activate the evacuation protocols, the Doctor and Sarah Jane helped the wounded and directed the defenders to the escape routes. The sounds of battle filled the air, a cacophony of destruction and death.

In the control room, the last line of defenders held their ground. Sheppard, Teyla, and the remaining soldiers fought with everything they had, determined to buy time for the evacuation. "We won't let them take Atlantis," Sheppard vowed, firing his weapon until it clicked empty.

A Dalek beam struck Sheppard in the chest, and he fell to the ground, blood pooling around him. Teyla, her shoulder bleeding, fought on, her face a mask of pain and fury. "For Atlantis!" she cried, taking down another Dalek before collapsing from her wounds.

The Doctor, seeing his friends fall, felt a surge of anger and sorrow. "We need to go, now!" he shouted, pulling Sarah Jane towards the escape route.

As the last of the defenders fell, the Daleks breached the control room. "EX-TER-MIN-ATE!" they chanted, their weapons firing indiscriminately.

Dr. Weir, the last to leave, looked back at the city she had fought so hard to protect. "We will return," she whispered, tears in her eyes, before following the Doctor and the others to safety.

In the Jumper Bay, the evacuation was chaotic but efficient. The wounded were loaded onto the Jumpers first, followed by the remaining personnel. The Doctor and Sarah Jane helped secure the doors as the Jumpers prepared for launch.

"We need to go, now!" McKay shouted, his face pale with fear and determination.

The Jumpers lifted off, exiting the city just as another explosion rocked Atlantis. The city, now overrun with Daleks, was a scene of devastation and despair.

As the Jumpers flew away, the Doctor looked back at the city, his heart heavy with the loss and destruction. "We'll be back," he vowed. "And we will defeat them."

Sarah Jane, sitting next to him, placed a comforting hand on his arm. "We will, Doctor. We'll find a way."

As the Jumpers flew towards safety, the team knew that the battle for Atlantis was far from over. The Daleks had won this round, but the fight was not yet finished. They would regroup, rebuild, and return to reclaim their home from the invaders.

The war for Atlantis had only just begun.

Chapter 10: Losses and Sacrifices

The escape from Atlantis had been a harrowing ordeal. The Jumper Bay, now a makeshift refuge, was filled with the wounded and the weary. The whine of the engines and the distant rumble of explosions from the besieged city filled the air, a grim reminder of the devastation left behind.

Inside one of the Jumpers, the Doctor and Sarah Jane moved among the injured, offering what comfort they could. Dr. Weir stood at the front, her expression one of grim determination despite the chaos around her.

"We've lost so many," she whispered, her voice breaking. "I don't know how we can recover from this."

The Doctor placed a reassuring hand on her shoulder. "Elizabeth, I know this is difficult, but we will find a way. Atlantis has faced incredible odds before, and it's still standing. We will make sure it stands again."

As they tended to the wounded, McKay approached, his face etched with grief and exhaustion. "We've managed to get most of the survivors out, but... the casualty list is long. Too long."

"How many?" Dr. Weir asked, her voice trembling.

"Over a hundred," McKay replied, his voice barely above a whisper. "And that's not counting the ones who are still missing or captured."

A heavy silence fell over the Jumper. The weight of their losses was palpable, each person lost a gaping wound in their hearts. Major Sheppard, critically injured but conscious, lay on a stretcher nearby, his eyes filled with pain.

Teyla, her shoulder bandaged, knelt beside him. "John, you need to rest."

"I can't," Sheppard replied, his voice weak but resolute. "We need to figure out a plan. We can't let the Daleks win."

The Doctor knelt beside Sheppard, his face serious. "John, you need to recover. We all need to regroup. There will be another battle, but we must be ready for it."

Sheppard's eyes met the Doctor's, and he nodded slowly. "Just... don't let them take Atlantis."

"We won't," the Doctor promised.

The sound of sobbing drew their attention. In a corner of the Jumper, a young soldier cradled the body of a fallen comrade, tears streaming down his face. Sarah Jane approached him, her heart aching for the young man.

"He was my best friend," the soldier choked out. "We joined the expedition together. I should have protected him."

Sarah Jane knelt beside him, placing a gentle hand on his shoulder. "You did everything you could. He knew you were there for him, and he would want you to keep fighting. To honor his memory."

The soldier nodded, his sobs subsiding as he clung to Sarah Jane's comforting words. She stayed with him, offering silent support as he mourned his friend.

Dr. Weir, seeing the grief of her people, felt her own resolve harden. "We can't let this break us. We will mourn our dead, but we will also honor them by continuing the fight. Atlantis is our home, and we will take it back."

Her words echoed through the Jumper, a rallying cry that reignited the spark of hope in their hearts. The team gathered, sharing quiet moments of grief and solidarity. They had lost so much, but their determination burned brighter than ever.

The Doctor, standing beside Dr. Weir, looked out at the devastated faces of the Atlantis personnel. "You are all incredibly brave," he said, his voice carrying strength and conviction. "And I promise you, we will find a way to defeat the Daleks. They have underestimated us, and that will be their downfall."

McKay, despite his exhaustion, found a spark of defiance. "We have the technology, and we have the knowledge. We just need to use it wisely."

Sheppard, his voice gaining strength, added, "And we have each other. We've faced impossible odds before, and we've come through stronger. This time will be no different."

Teyla, her warrior spirit undiminished, stood tall. "We fight for those we have lost, and for those who still live. Atlantis is not just a city; it is a symbol of hope and resilience."

The Doctor nodded, his eyes meeting each of theirs in turn. "Together, we are more than the sum of our parts. We will reclaim Atlantis, and we will show the Daleks that they cannot destroy the spirit of this place."

Dr. Weir, feeling the strength of her team around her, took a deep breath. "Then let's start planning. We need to regroup, resupply, and prepare for the counterattack. The Daleks have taken our home, but they will not keep it."

As the team began to strategize, the sound of explosions and the sight of smoke rising from Atlantis served as a stark reminder of the battle ahead. But within the Jumper, a sense of unity and resolve grew stronger. They were not just fighting for a city; they were fighting for their fallen comrades, for their future, and for the very essence of Atlantis.

The Doctor, Sarah Jane, Dr. Weir, McKay, Sheppard, Teyla, and the remaining Atlantis personnel stood united in their grief and determination. The losses they had suffered would fuel their resolve, and the sacrifices made would not be in vain. The battle for Atlantis was far from over, and they were ready to fight with everything they had.

Chapter 11: Ancient Secrets Revealed

The mood in the Jumper was somber but focused. After taking stock of their losses and renewing their resolve, the Atlantis team knew they had to act swiftly. The Doctor had a hunch that the answers they needed might be hidden within the vast archives of Atlantis.

"There's a section of the Ancient archives we haven't fully explored," the Doctor explained to Dr. Weir and McKay. "If the Daleks are here, they might be after something specific."

Dr. Weir nodded. "The Ancients' knowledge is vast. If the Daleks are trying to harness their technology, it could be catastrophic."

"Then let's not waste any time," McKay said, already moving towards the Jumper's control console. "We need to access those archives and find out what the Daleks are planning."

The Jumper glided through the ruins of Atlantis, avoiding the areas still swarming with Daleks. They landed near a hidden entrance to the city's underground archives. The team moved quickly, navigating the labyrinthine corridors lit by flickering emergency lights.

Inside the archives, the Doctor and McKay worked side by side, scanning through ancient data banks and holographic records. The air was thick with the hum of old machinery coming back to life.

"Look at this," the Doctor said, pointing to a series of holographic schematics. "The Daleks have been accessing these files. They're after something called the 'Chrono Nexus'."

"Chrono Nexus?" McKay echoed, tapping furiously on his tablet. "Let me cross-reference that with the database."

As McKay deciphered the data, Sarah Jane, Sheppard, and Teyla stood guard, their weapons ready for any Dalek patrols. The tension in the air was palpable, everyone aware of the high stakes.

"Got it!" McKay exclaimed, his face paling as he read the information. "The Chrono Nexus is a temporal device. It can manipulate time on a massive scale. If the Daleks get their hands on this, they could rewrite history, conquer entire civilizations before they even develop defenses."

Dr. Weir's face hardened. "That's why they came to Atlantis. The Ancients must have developed this technology, and the Daleks want to use it for their own ends."

The Doctor's eyes narrowed. "We can't let that happen. If the Daleks gain control of time itself, they'll be unstoppable. We need to find and secure the Chrono Nexus before they do."

Sarah Jane stepped forward, her expression determined. "How do we find it? And more importantly, how do we stop them?"

McKay pulled up a detailed map of Atlantis. "According to the archives, the Chrono Nexus is located in a hidden chamber beneath the central spire. It's heavily guarded by ancient security systems."

Sheppard cracked a smile. "Sounds like a challenge. But we've faced worse."

The Doctor nodded, his face resolute. "Indeed. We need to move quickly. The longer we wait, the closer the Daleks get to finding it."

Teyla, her eyes scanning the corridor, added, "We should expect heavy resistance. The Daleks won't give up easily."

As the team prepared to move out, the Doctor paused, his mind racing. "Elizabeth, Rodney, you'll need to coordinate our efforts from here. Access any additional data you can find on the Chrono Nexus. We need to know exactly what we're dealing with."

Dr. Weir nodded. "Understood. We'll do everything we can to support you."

McKay, his skepticism replaced by a fierce determination, added, "And Doctor, be careful. We can't afford to lose you."

The Doctor smiled briefly. "Don't worry, Rodney. I've faced the Daleks before, and I'll face them again. We'll get through this."

With a final nod, the Doctor, Sarah Jane, Sheppard, and Teyla set off towards the hidden chamber. The corridors of Atlantis were eerily silent, the occasional distant explosion reminding them of the ongoing battle.

As they approached the entrance to the chamber, they encountered a squad of Daleks. "IN-TRU-DERS WILL BE EX-TER-MIN-ATED!" the Daleks chanted, their weapons charging.

"Take cover!" Sheppard shouted, firing his P-90 at the advancing Daleks. The corridor erupted into chaos, energy beams and bullets flying in every direction.

Teyla, using her agility and combat prowess, dodged a Dalek beam and launched herself at another, disabling it with a precise strike. Sarah Jane, armed with an energy pistol, fired at a Dalek's eyestalk, temporarily blinding it.

The Doctor, using his sonic screwdriver, created an electromagnetic pulse that disrupted the Daleks' systems. "Now! Hit them hard!" he yelled.

Sheppard and Teyla took down the remaining Daleks, their combined efforts proving too much for the mechanical menaces. The corridor fell silent once more, the air thick with the smell of scorched metal.

"We can't afford any more delays," the Doctor said, his voice urgent. "Let's move."

They reached the entrance to the hidden chamber, a massive door inscribed with ancient symbols. "This is it," McKay's voice crackled over the comms. "The Chrono Nexus should be inside."

The Doctor examined the door, his brow furrowed in concentration. "It's protected by a complex locking mechanism. Stand back."

Using his sonic screwdriver, the Doctor manipulated the ancient locks, the door slowly creaking open to reveal a vast chamber bathed in a soft, blue light. In the center of the room stood the Chrono Nexus, a crystalline structure pulsating with temporal energy.

"We found it," Sarah Jane breathed, her eyes wide with awe.

But their victory was short-lived. As they stepped into the chamber, a squad of Daleks materialized, their weapons trained on the team. "EX-TER-MIN-ATE! EX-TER-MIN-ATE!"

"Take cover!" Sheppard shouted, diving behind a pillar as the Daleks opened fire.

The Doctor, realizing the danger, shouted, "We need to protect the Chrono Nexus at all costs! If the Daleks get their hands on it, they'll destroy everything!"

As the battle raged in the chamber, the team fought with everything they had. Teyla's swift movements and Sheppard's precise shots took down several Daleks, but the enemy kept coming.

Sarah Jane, seeing an opportunity, grabbed a fallen Dalek weapon and fired at the control panel on the wall, causing an explosion that disrupted the Daleks' formation. "Doctor, now's your chance!"

The Doctor rushed to the Chrono Nexus, using his sonic screwdriver to interface with its systems. "I'm setting it to overload. If we can't have it, neither can they."

The room shook violently as the Chrono Nexus began to pulse with increasing energy. The Daleks, realizing the danger, tried to retreat, but the team held their ground, preventing any escape.

"Doctor, we need to get out of here!" Sheppard yelled, covering the Doctor as he worked.

"Just a few more seconds!" the Doctor shouted back, his fingers flying over the controls.

With a final surge of energy, the Chrono Nexus overloaded, sending a shockwave through the chamber. The Daleks were caught in the blast, their metallic shells shattering as the temporal energy tore through them.

"Everyone, out!" the Doctor shouted, grabbing Sarah Jane's hand and pulling her towards the exit.

The team barely made it out of the chamber as it collapsed behind them, sealing the Chrono Nexus and the remaining Daleks inside. They stumbled into the corridor, breathless but alive.

"We did it," Teyla said, her voice filled with relief. "The Daleks won't be able to use the Chrono Nexus now."

The Doctor, his face smeared with dirt and sweat, nodded. "Yes, but we need to make sure they can't rebuild. We have to keep fighting."

Dr. Weir's voice came over the comms. "Doctor, what's your status?"

"We secured the Chrono Nexus," the Doctor replied. "The Daleks can't use it. But we need to regroup and plan our next move."

"Understood," Dr. Weir said, her voice filled with relief and determination. "We'll be ready. Atlantis will not fall."

As the team made their way back to the Jumper, the Doctor looked at his companions, their faces reflecting the hardship and hope of their mission. They had uncovered the Daleks' plan and thwarted it, but the fight was far from over. They would continue to battle for Atlantis, no matter the cost.

Chapter 12: Rallying the Troops

Back in the relative safety of the Jumper Bay, the Atlantis team gathered to assess their situation. The tension was palpable, but there was also a steely determination in the air. Major Sheppard, despite his injuries, stood before the assembled personnel, ready to rally the troops for what could be their final stand.

"Listen up, everyone," Sheppard began, his voice strong despite the pain. "We've taken a beating, but we're not done yet. The Daleks have thrown everything they've got at us, and we're still here. Now, it's our turn to hit back."

The soldiers and civilians around him nodded, their faces a mix of fear and resolve. Teyla stepped forward, her presence commanding attention. "We fight not just for Atlantis, but for each other. For our friends and family. For the fallen. We will not let the Daleks take what is ours."

The crowd murmured in agreement, their spirits lifting. The Doctor, standing beside Sarah Jane and McKay, knew it was time to inspire the team with the resolve they needed. He stepped forward, his eyes sweeping over the faces of the people who looked to him for guidance.

"Everyone," the Doctor began, his voice calm and steady, "we are facing one of the greatest threats the universe has ever known. The Daleks are relentless, merciless, and they believe themselves to be unstoppable. But they are wrong."

He paused, letting his words sink in. "You are the defenders of Atlantis, a city built on the legacy of the Ancients. A city that has withstood the test of time and countless threats. And today, you stand united against this new enemy."

The crowd listened intently, hanging on his every word. "The Daleks think they can break us, but they underestimate the strength of unity, the power of resilience. Each of you is a vital part of this team, and together, we can achieve the impossible."

Sarah Jane stepped forward, adding her voice to the Doctor's. "We've faced impossible odds before, and we've come through stronger. We are more than just individuals; we are a family, a community. And we will fight for our home, for our future."

McKay, though usually skeptical of motivational speeches, felt the energy in the room shift. "We've got the technology, the knowledge, and the will to win this. We just need to stand together and use every resource we have."

Dr. Weir, standing at the back of the room, took a deep breath and stepped forward to address the group. "Our priority is to protect our civilians and secure essential facilities. Medical personnel, engineers, and scientists—your job is to keep our support systems running. Security teams, coordinate with Major Sheppard and Teyla. We need to fortify our defenses and prepare for the next wave."

She turned to the Doctor, a look of gratitude and determination in her eyes. "Doctor, your knowledge and experience are invaluable. Guide us, and we will follow."

The Doctor nodded, his eyes filled with resolve. "Let's get to work."

The team dispersed, each member heading to their assigned tasks with renewed vigor. Sheppard and Teyla began organizing the remaining soldiers and security personnel, mapping out defensive positions and setting up barricades.

"Alright, I want teams positioned at every major access point," Sheppard instructed, pointing to a map of Atlantis. "We need to create chokepoints and control the flow of any Dalek advance. Use the terrain to our advantage."

Teyla added, "Ensure that all entrances are fortified. We must be prepared for both frontal assaults and flanking maneuvers. Stay alert and communicate any movements immediately."

As the soldiers moved to implement their plans, Dr. Weir coordinated with the medical and engineering teams. "We need to secure the medical bay and ensure we have supplies for the wounded. Engineers, focus on maintaining our power systems and repairing any critical infrastructure. We can't afford any failures."

The Doctor and McKay worked together to enhance the city's defenses using the remaining Ancient technology. "If we can reroute power from non-essential systems, we might be able to boost the shield strength," McKay suggested, his mind racing with possibilities.

"Good idea," the Doctor agreed. "And if we can integrate the drone technology into our defensive grid, we'll have a more robust response to their attacks."

Sarah Jane assisted where she could, offering words of encouragement and helping to organize the efforts. "We're all in this together," she said to a group of young engineers. "Every contribution counts."

As the preparations continued, the Doctor gathered the key leaders in the central control room. "We need to be ready for anything. The Daleks won't give up easily, and we have to be prepared for their counterattacks."

Dr. Weir nodded, her face set with determination. "We'll be ready. The people of Atlantis are stronger than they know."

The Doctor smiled, a glimmer of hope in his eyes. "And we'll remind the Daleks of that strength."

The room fell silent for a moment, each person lost in their thoughts of the coming battle. The stakes were higher than ever, but the sense of unity and purpose was stronger too.

"To victory," Sheppard said, raising his weapon in a salute.

"To Atlantis," Teyla echoed, her voice filled with resolve.

"To each other," Sarah Jane added, her eyes meeting the Doctor's.

The Doctor nodded, his face serious but hopeful. "To the future."

With their hearts steeled and their resolve unwavering, the team of Atlantis prepared for the final stand against the Daleks. They knew the road ahead would be fraught with danger and sacrifice, but they also knew that together, they were capable of extraordinary things.

As the countdown to the next wave began, the defenders of Atlantis stood united, ready to face whatever came their way. Their home, their future, and their very survival depended on their courage and their unity. And with the Doctor by their side, they felt ready to face even the most impossible odds.

Chapter 13: The Final Stand

The preparations were complete. The defenders of Atlantis were in position, their makeshift fortifications ready, their weapons charged, and their spirits steeled for the coming battle. The tension was palpable, the air thick with the anticipation of what lay ahead. The Daleks would not stop until they had conquered Atlantis, but the team was determined to fight with everything they had.

Major Sheppard and Teyla stood at the forefront of the defensive line, their eyes scanning the horizon for any sign of the enemy. The Doctor, Sarah Jane, McKay, and Dr. Weir were positioned in the central control room, coordinating the final assault.

"Alright, everyone," Sheppard's voice crackled over the comms. "This is it. Remember your training, remember what you're fighting for. We hold this line at all costs."

Teyla nodded, her expression resolute. "Stay strong, stay focused. We will not let the Daleks take our home."

The Doctor, his mind racing with strategies and contingencies, addressed the control room. "We need to hit them hard and fast. Our goal is to disrupt their command structure and take out their leader. Without their leader, the Dalek forces will be in disarray."

McKay, his fingers flying over the console, added, "I've integrated the drone technology into our defensive grid. It should give us an edge, but we need to be smart about it. We can't afford to waste any resources."

Dr. Weir, her face set with determination, turned to the Doctor. "What do you need us to do?"

The Doctor's eyes met hers. "I'll lead a small team to confront the Dalek leader. We need to create a diversion to draw their attention away from the control room. If we can get close enough, we can disable their command center and take out their leader."

Sarah Jane stepped forward, her eyes filled with resolve. "I'll go with you, Doctor. We need to end this."

The Doctor nodded, his heart swelling with pride and determination. "Alright. Sheppard, Teyla, hold the line and keep the Daleks occupied. We'll take care of the leader."

With the plan set, the team moved into action. The sound of the approaching Dalek forces grew louder, their metallic voices echoing through the corridors of Atlantis. "EX-TER-MIN-ATE! EX-TER-MIN-ATE!"

The first wave of Daleks breached the outer defenses, and the battle began in earnest. Energy beams and bullets filled the air, the clash of weapons and the cries of the wounded creating a cacophony of chaos and destruction.

Sheppard led his team with fierce determination, his weapon blazing as he took down one Dalek after another. "Hold the line! Don't let them through!"

Teyla moved with deadly grace, her combat skills unmatched as she disabled and destroyed the advancing Daleks. "For Atlantis!" she cried, her voice a rallying call for the defenders.

In the control room, the Doctor, Sarah Jane, and a small team of elite soldiers prepared for their mission. "Stay close and move fast," the Doctor instructed. "We can't afford to be caught in the crossfire."

They slipped through the corridors, avoiding the main battle as they made their way to the Dalek command center. The sound of explosions and the cries of the wounded echoed around them, a grim reminder of the stakes.

As they approached the command center, the Doctor used his sonic screwdriver to disable the security systems. "We're in. Move quickly and stay alert."

Inside the command center, they found the Dalek leader, a larger and more formidable version of the standard Dalek, surrounded by its elite guard. "IN-TRU-DERS WILL BE EX-TER-MIN-ATED!" the Dalek leader screeched, its weapon charging.

"Now!" the Doctor shouted, and the team launched their attack.

The battle was intense and brutal. The elite Daleks were faster and more powerful, but the Atlantis team fought with unmatched determination. Energy beams and explosions filled the air as the two sides clashed.

Sarah Jane, using her agility and quick thinking, managed to disable one of the elite Daleks with a well-placed shot to its eyestalk. "Doctor, we need to take out the leader now!"

The Doctor, dodging a barrage of energy beams, focused his sonic screwdriver on the Dalek leader. "Cover me!"

The soldiers formed a protective barrier around the Doctor, firing relentlessly at the elite Daleks to keep them at bay. The Doctor's sonic screwdriver whirred and buzzed as he worked to disable the Dalek leader's command functions.

"IN-SUFFICIENT DATA! COMMAND STRUC-TURE FAIL-ING!" the Dalek leader screeched, its systems faltering.

With a final surge of energy, the Doctor disabled the Dalek leader, causing it to collapse in a heap of sparking metal. The remaining elite Daleks, now leaderless, were quickly dispatched by the Atlantis team.

"We did it," Sarah Jane breathed, her heart pounding. "We actually did it."

The Doctor, his face smeared with sweat and grime, nodded. "It's not over yet. We need to get back to the control room and make sure the rest of the Dalek forces are dealt with."

They hurried back through the corridors, the sounds of battle still raging around them. When they reached the control room, they found that Sheppard and Teyla had managed to hold the line, but the cost had been high. The room was filled with the injured and the dead, the survivors grimly holding their positions.

"The leader is down," the Doctor announced. "The Dalek forces should be in disarray. Now's our chance to push them back."

McKay, his face pale but determined, nodded. "I've got the drones ready. We can launch a full-scale counterattack."

Dr. Weir, her eyes filled with a mix of relief and sorrow, addressed the remaining defenders. "This is our moment. We push back the Daleks and reclaim Atlantis. For our fallen comrades, for our home, for the future."

The defenders rallied, their spirits lifted by the news. The drones launched into the air, their energy beams targeting the remaining Dalek forces with deadly precision. The combined efforts of the Atlantis team and the drone technology proved too much for the disorganized Daleks.

As the last of the Daleks were destroyed, a cheer rose from the defenders. They had done it. They had defended Atlantis and defeated the Dalek invasion.

The Doctor, standing amidst the ruins of the control room, felt a surge of pride and relief. He turned to Dr. Weir, Sarah Jane, McKay, Sheppard, and Teyla, his eyes filled with gratitude. "We did it. Together, we saved Atlantis."

Dr. Weir nodded, her eyes brimming with tears. "Thank you, Doctor. We couldn't have done it without you."

The Doctor shook his head. "It was all of us, Elizabeth. Every single person here played a part. This victory belongs to all of us."

As the survivors began to tend to the wounded and assess the damage, the Doctor looked out over the city. The battle had been won, but the scars of the conflict would remain. Yet, in that moment, there was hope. Hope for a future where Atlantis would stand strong and proud, a beacon of resilience and unity.

And as the sun set over the battered city, the defenders of Atlantis knew that they had faced the darkness and emerged victorious. They had proven that even in the face of impossible odds, the spirit of Atlantis would never be broken.

Chapter 14: Showdown with the Daleks

The remnants of the Dalek forces were retreating, but the Doctor knew their true leader, the Dalek Supreme, had yet to be confronted. This final confrontation would determine the fate of Atlantis. As the team regrouped, the Doctor prepared them for what lay ahead.

"The Dalek Supreme is still out there," the Doctor said, his voice grim but resolute. "We need to face it head-on. This is our final battle."

Sarah Jane stepped forward, determination in her eyes. "We're with you, Doctor. All the way."

Teyla, her weapons ready, nodded. "We fight together. For Atlantis."

The Doctor, Sarah Jane, Teyla, and a small team of elite soldiers made their way through the war-torn corridors of Atlantis. The Dalek Supreme had established its command center in the heart of the city, using the Ancient technology to its advantage. They moved quickly and silently, knowing that any hesitation could be fatal.

As they approached the command center, the Doctor signaled for them to halt. "We need to be careful. The Dalek Supreme is more dangerous than any we've faced before. It will be heavily guarded."

Teyla, her eyes scanning the surroundings, added, "We must strike quickly and decisively. Any delay could cost us dearly."

The Doctor nodded. "Alright, let's move."

They entered the command center, a vast room filled with Dalek machinery and glowing consoles. At the center stood the Dalek Supreme, its black and gold casing gleaming ominously. Surrounding it were several elite Daleks, their weapons trained on the intruders.

"DOCTOR!" the Dalek Supreme's voice boomed, filled with venom and malice. "YOU WILL BE EX-TER-MIN-ATED!"

"Not today," the Doctor replied, stepping forward with a confident smile. "You've underestimated us, Dalek Supreme. This ends now."

The Dalek Supreme's eyestalk swiveled, its voice cold and calculating. "YOU ARE WEAK, DOCTOR. YOU CANNOT DEFEAT THE DALEKS. WE ARE SUPREME!"

The Doctor's smile widened. "We'll see about that. Everyone, now!"

The battle erupted in a flurry of energy beams and gunfire. Sarah Jane and Teyla moved with precision and skill, their combat training evident as they took down the elite Daleks one by one. Sarah Jane, using her energy pistol, targeted the Daleks' eyestalks, temporarily blinding them and making them vulnerable. Teyla, with her combination of martial arts and energy weapons, moved like a whirlwind, striking with deadly accuracy.

The Doctor, meanwhile, focused on the Dalek Supreme. Using his sonic screwdriver, he began to interface with the Dalek machinery, attempting to disable its systems. "You're clever, Dalek Supreme, but I've faced worse than you."

"YOU WILL FAIL, DOCTOR!" the Dalek Supreme screeched, firing its weapon. The Doctor dodged the beam, continuing his work.

As the elite Daleks fell, the Dalek Supreme grew more agitated. "ALL DALEKS, CONVERGE ON THE COMMAND CENTER! EX-TER-MIN-ATE THE IN-TRU-DERS!"

The Doctor glanced at Sarah Jane and Teyla. "We need to take it down now!"

Sarah Jane, dodging a beam, shouted, "Doctor, over here! There's a power conduit exposed!"

The Doctor saw the conduit, realizing its significance. "Brilliant, Sarah Jane! If we overload it, we can create a feedback loop that will disable the Dalek Supreme."

Teyla provided cover as the Doctor and Sarah Jane moved towards the conduit. "I'll hold them off! Do it quickly!"

The Doctor used his sonic screwdriver to manipulate the power conduit, causing it to spark and hum with energy. "Almost there... just a bit more..."

The Dalek Supreme, sensing the danger, fired relentlessly. "YOU WILL NOT SUCCEED! THE DALEKS ARE SUPREME!"

"Not today," the Doctor muttered, completing the final adjustments. "Sarah Jane, now!"

Sarah Jane fired her energy pistol at the conduit, causing a massive explosion. The feedback loop surged through the Dalek Supreme, its systems going into overload. "MALFUNCTION! MALFUNCTION! SYS-TEMS FAIL-ING!"

The Doctor, pulling Sarah Jane to safety, watched as the Dalek Supreme convulsed, its casing sparking and cracking. "This is for all the lives you've taken," he said, his voice filled with quiet fury.

With a final, ear-splitting screech, the Dalek Supreme exploded, its remains scattered across the command center. The remaining Daleks, now leaderless and disorganized, were quickly dispatched by Teyla and the soldiers.

The room fell silent, the only sound the crackle of burning machinery. The Doctor, Sarah Jane, and Teyla stood amidst the wreckage, their breaths coming in heavy gasps.

"We did it," Sarah Jane said, her voice filled with relief and exhaustion. "It's over."

The Doctor nodded, his face a mixture of triumph and sorrow. "Yes, but the cost was high. So many lives lost."

Teyla, her expression resolute, stepped forward. "We honor their memory by ensuring that Atlantis remains free. They did not die in vain."

The Doctor placed a hand on her shoulder. "You're right, Teyla. We fought for Atlantis, and we won. Now, we rebuild."

As they made their way back to the central control room, the weight of their victory settled over them. The battle had been fierce, and the losses great, but they had triumphed against one of the most formidable enemies in the universe.

In the control room, Dr. Weir, McKay, and the remaining team members awaited their return. As the Doctor, Sarah Jane, and Teyla entered, a cheer rose from the assembled personnel.

"We heard the explosion," Dr. Weir said, her eyes shining with pride. "You did it."

The Doctor nodded. "The Dalek Supreme is no more. The remaining Dalek forces are disorganized and retreating. We have won."

McKay, his usual skepticism replaced with genuine admiration, stepped forward. "You saved us, Doctor. All of you. Thank you."

The Doctor, ever humble, shook his head. "We saved each other. Atlantis is a symbol of what we can achieve when we stand together."

Dr. Weir raised her voice, addressing the entire room. "Today, we faced a great threat and emerged victorious. We mourn our losses, but we celebrate our resilience. Atlantis stands because of each and every one of you. Thank you."

The room erupted in applause, the sound echoing through the corridors of Atlantis. They had faced the darkness and emerged into the light, stronger and more united than ever.

As the sun set over the city, the defenders of Atlantis knew that they had achieved something extraordinary. They had confronted the Dalek menace and triumphed. The future was theirs to shape, and they would do so with the same courage and determination that had seen them through the darkest of times.

The Doctor, standing with Sarah Jane, Teyla, Sheppard, McKay, and Dr. Weir, felt a profound sense of hope. Atlantis had endured, and so would they. Together, they would face whatever challenges lay ahead, united by their shared purpose and unwavering resolve.

Chapter 15: Turning the Tide

The battle in the command center had given Atlantis a glimmer of hope, but the struggle was far from over. The Daleks, though disorganized, were still a formidable force, and they would not retreat easily. The Doctor knew they needed a decisive move to turn the tide fully in their favor.

Back in the central control room, the Doctor gathered the key leaders. "The Dalek Supreme's destruction has thrown their forces into chaos, but we need to capitalize on this advantage quickly. McKay, how are we on reactivating the Ancient drone chair?"

McKay, still bruised and battered from the earlier skirmishes, was busy at the console. "I've rerouted power and bypassed several corrupted circuits. It's almost ready. We just need to synchronize the drone control systems."

"Good," the Doctor said, his voice filled with urgency. "The drones will give us the firepower we need to drive the Daleks out of the city. We need to launch a coordinated counterattack and push them back."

Dr. Weir, standing nearby, nodded. "I'll coordinate our remaining forces. We need to protect our key facilities and civilians while we launch this counteroffensive."

Sarah Jane, her eyes filled with determination, stepped forward. "I'll help with the evacuation and defense efforts. We need to keep everyone safe."

The Doctor placed a reassuring hand on her shoulder. "Thank you, Sarah Jane. Your help is invaluable."

Teyla, still recovering from her injuries but determined to fight, addressed the assembled soldiers. "We must stand strong and fight with all we have. This is our home, and we will not let the Daleks take it from us."

Major Sheppard, his injuries bandaged but his spirit unbroken, added, "Alright, people. This is it. We push them back and take back our city. Stay sharp and watch each other's backs."

As the team prepared for the final push, McKay continued his work on the drone chair. The Doctor assisted, using his sonic screwdriver to fine-tune the synchronization process. "We need to make sure the drones can target the Daleks accurately," he explained.

McKay nodded, his focus unwavering. "I'm on it. Just a few more adjustments..."

Suddenly, the room's lights flickered, and the drone chair hummed to life. "It's ready!" McKay announced, a mix of relief and triumph in his voice.

The Doctor quickly took his place in the chair, his hands moving over the controls. "Alright, let's see what these drones can do."

The drones, sleek and deadly, launched from their hidden compartments throughout the city. They soared into the air, their energy beams targeting the Dalek forces with precision and power. The counterattack had begun.

The defenders of Atlantis watched in awe as the drones tore through the Dalek ranks, their beams cutting down the enemy with ruthless efficiency. "It's working!" Sheppard shouted over the comms. "The drones are pushing them back!"

Teyla, fighting alongside her fellow soldiers, saw the Daleks falter and begin to retreat. "Keep up the pressure! Do not let them regroup!"

In the control room, the Doctor and McKay coordinated the drone strikes, targeting key Dalek positions and maximizing their effectiveness. "We need to hit their command nodes," the Doctor said. "It will further disrupt their coordination."

McKay adjusted the targeting parameters. "Got it. Sending the drones to target those nodes now."

The drones, guided by the precise commands from the control room, struck the Dalek command nodes, causing explosions and further disarray among the enemy ranks. The Daleks, realizing their precarious situation, began a hasty retreat.

"Dalek forces are retreating!" Dr. Weir reported, her voice filled with cautious optimism. "We're turning the tide!"

But the victory was not yet secure. The Daleks, in a final desperate assault, launched a concentrated attack on the central control room. "They're coming for us!" a soldier shouted, his weapon ready.

The control room shuddered as the first wave of Daleks breached the outer defenses. "We need to hold them off!" the Doctor shouted. "McKay, keep the drones on them!"

McKay's fingers flew over the console. "I'm doing my best, but we need more time!"

Sarah Jane and Teyla took up defensive positions, their weapons blazing as the Daleks poured into the room. The battle was fierce, the air filled with the sounds of energy beams and gunfire.

"EX-TER-MIN-ATE!" the Daleks chanted, their relentless advance threatening to overwhelm the defenders.

"We need to push them back!" Sheppard shouted, rallying his troops. "Don't let them through!"

The Doctor, realizing the urgency of the situation, activated a secondary defense mechanism within the drone chair. "McKay, reroute power to the internal defense grid!"

McKay, his face strained with concentration, complied. "Done! Activating now!"

Energy barriers sprang to life around the control room, providing a temporary shield against the Dalek onslaught. The drones, directed by the Doctor, intensified their attacks, targeting the remaining Dalek forces with unerring accuracy.

The combined efforts of the drones and the defenders began to turn the tide. The Daleks, their numbers dwindling and their leaderless ranks in disarray, were pushed back. "They're retreating!" Teyla shouted, her voice filled with fierce determination.

As the last of the Daleks were driven from the control room, the defenders let out a cheer. They had held their ground and pushed the enemy back.

The Doctor, stepping down from the drone chair, looked around at the weary but victorious faces. "We did it. Atlantis stands."

Dr. Weir, her eyes brimming with tears of relief and pride, approached the Doctor. "Thank you, Doctor. You saved us."

The Doctor shook his head. "We saved each other. This victory belongs to everyone here."

Sarah Jane, her face flushed with the thrill of battle, hugged the Doctor. "You were brilliant, as always."

The Doctor smiled, his eyes twinkling. "And so were you, Sarah Jane. All of you."

As the team began to assess the damage and tend to the wounded, the realization of their victory settled over them. They had faced the Daleks and emerged triumphant. The cost had been high, but Atlantis had survived.

The Doctor, looking out over the battered city, felt a profound sense of hope. The battle had been won, but the work was far from over. Together, they would rebuild and ensure that Atlantis remained a beacon of resilience and strength.

And as the first light of dawn broke over the horizon, the defenders of Atlantis knew that they had turned the tide. They had faced the darkness and emerged victorious, united by their courage and determination. The future was theirs to shape, and they would do so with the same unwavering resolve that had seen them through the darkest of times.

Chapter 16: Betrayal and Redemption

The euphoria of their recent victory was short-lived. As the team worked tirelessly to fortify their defenses and tend to the wounded, an unexpected threat lurked within their ranks. Unbeknownst to the defenders of Atlantis, the Daleks had left behind a more insidious weapon—a sleeper agent, programmed to sow discord and chaos from within.

In the central control room, the Doctor, Dr. Weir, Sheppard, McKay, Teyla, and Sarah Jane were planning their next moves. The air was filled with a mix of relief and tension, everyone acutely aware that the Daleks could strike again at any moment.

"We need to ensure that all our systems are secure and operational," Dr. Weir said, her eyes scanning the room. "Rodney, can you run a full diagnostic on our defense grid?"

McKay nodded, already typing furiously on his tablet. "On it. I'll make sure everything is running smoothly."

As the team dispersed to their tasks, a sudden alarm blared through the control room. "Unauthorized access detected in the main server room!" a technician shouted, his voice tinged with panic.

Sheppard immediately grabbed his weapon. "Let's move. Doctor, you're with me."

The Doctor nodded, his face grim. "Let's find out what's going on."

They rushed through the corridors, their hearts pounding with the urgency of the alarm. As they approached the server room, the door slid open to reveal a member of the Atlantis team, frantically working at a console. It was Lieutenant Kavanagh, his face pale and eyes wild.

"Kavanagh, what are you doing?" Sheppard demanded, raising his weapon.

Kavanagh turned, his expression one of desperation. "You don't understand! I had no choice!"

The Doctor's eyes narrowed. "Kavanagh, step away from the console."

But before Kavanagh could comply, his eyes glazed over, and his voice took on a mechanical tone. "I AM UNDER ORDERS. YOU WILL NOT INTERFERE."

"He's been compromised," the Doctor realized, his voice filled with urgency. "He's under Dalek control!"

Kavanagh's hand moved to a concealed device on his belt, a small, pulsing sphere. "SELF-DESTRUCT INITIATED. YOU WILL BE EX-TER-MIN-ATED."

"Get down!" Sheppard shouted, tackling the Doctor to the ground just as Kavanagh pressed the button. The device exploded, sending a shockwave through the room. Kavanagh was thrown against the wall, the force of the blast knocking him unconscious.

The Doctor and Sheppard, dazed but unharmed, quickly got to their feet. "We need to get him to the infirmary," the Doctor said, checking Kavanagh's pulse. "He might have information we can use."

They carried Kavanagh to the infirmary, where Dr. Beckett and his medical team immediately began treating him. "What happened?" Beckett asked, his eyes wide with concern.

"He was under Dalek control," the Doctor explained. "We need to find out what they did to him and if there's any way to reverse it."

Beckett nodded, his expression grim. "I'll do what I can."

As Kavanagh was stabilized and placed under observation, the Doctor and Sheppard returned to the control room. The mood was tense, everyone aware of the potential threat from within.

"We need to ensure this doesn't happen again," Dr. Weir said, her voice steady but strained. "Doctor, can you identify how the Daleks were able to control Kavanagh?"

The Doctor nodded. "I'll need to examine the device he used. There might be a way to trace the signal back to its source."

McKay, his face pale but determined, spoke up. "I'll help. We need to understand their technology if we're going to protect ourselves."

As they worked, the Doctor and McKay discovered a series of encoded transmissions embedded in the device. "This is it," the Doctor said, his eyes narrowing. "These transmissions are how the Daleks controlled him. If we can decode them, we might be able to find a weakness in their system."

Hours passed as the Doctor and McKay pored over the data, their minds racing to unravel the Dalek code. Finally, McKay's eyes lit up. "I've got it! There's a pattern here. The Daleks are using a specific frequency to communicate with their agents."

The Doctor smiled, a glint of triumph in his eyes. "And if we can disrupt that frequency, we can neutralize their control."

Dr. Weir, standing nearby, listened intently. "Can we use this to our advantage?"

The Doctor nodded. "Yes. If we can transmit a counter-signal, we can not only free anyone under Dalek control but also potentially disrupt their entire command network."

Sheppard, his face set with determination, added, "Let's do it. We need to hit them where it hurts."

The team quickly mobilized, setting up the necessary equipment to transmit the counter-signal. As the signal was broadcast, a ripple of energy spread through Atlantis, targeting the hidden Dalek frequencies.

Back in the infirmary, Kavanagh stirred, his eyes fluttering open. "What... what happened?" he murmured, his voice weak.

The Doctor leaned over him, a reassuring smile on his face. "You're safe now. The Daleks can't control you anymore."

Kavanagh's eyes filled with tears. "I didn't mean to... I couldn't stop it. They were inside my head."

"It's alright," the Doctor said gently. "You're free now. And you've given us the information we need to fight back."

Kavanagh's actions, though initially causing chaos, had inadvertently provided the team with a crucial advantage. The counter-signal disrupted the Dalek control network, giving the defenders of Atlantis a chance to regroup and strengthen their defenses.

As the team gathered to assess the situation, Dr. Weir addressed them. "Today, we faced a threat from within, but we also discovered a way to strike back at the Daleks. We stand together, stronger than ever. Thank you for your bravery and resilience."

The Doctor, standing beside her, added, "We have the knowledge and the technology to turn the tide. The Daleks will not prevail. Atlantis will endure."

The room filled with a sense of renewed hope and determination. They had faced betrayal and emerged stronger, their unity and resolve unwavering.

As they prepared for the next phase of their battle, the defenders of Atlantis knew that they had the tools and the spirit to overcome any challenge. They would continue to fight, to protect their home and their future, united in their shared purpose and unbreakable bond.

And with the Doctor by their side, they felt ready to face whatever the Daleks might throw at them next. The fight for Atlantis was far from over, but they were more determined than ever to ensure their victory.

Chapter 17: Race Against Time

The success of the counter-signal had given the team a crucial edge, but the Dalek threat was far from neutralized. The Doctor and McKay knew they needed to act swiftly to implement their final plan to disable the Dalek fleet once and for all. The clock was ticking, and every second counted.

In the central control room, the team gathered for a final briefing. The atmosphere was charged with urgency and determination. The Doctor stood at the center, a holographic map of Atlantis and the surrounding space displayed before him.

"Alright, everyone," the Doctor began, his voice steady but urgent. "We've managed to disrupt their control network, but the Daleks are regrouping. We need to disable their fleet before they can launch another full-scale assault."

McKay stepped forward, his face pale but resolute. "We've identified a key weakness in their fleet's central command structure. If we can infiltrate their main control ship and plant a disruption device, we can disable their entire fleet."

Dr. Weir nodded, her expression serious. "What do you need from us?"

"We'll need a diversion," the Doctor replied. "Something to draw the Daleks' attention away from the control ship. Sheppard, Teyla, can you coordinate a strike on their forward positions?"

Sheppard, his injuries bandaged but his spirit unbroken, nodded. "Consider it done. We'll keep them busy."

Teyla, standing beside him, added, "We will do whatever it takes to give you the time you need."

The Doctor turned to Sarah Jane. "Sarah, you'll be with us. We need your skills and your bravery for this mission."

Sarah Jane nodded, her eyes filled with determination. "Let's do it."

With the plan set, the team moved into action. Sheppard and Teyla led a group of soldiers to create a diversion, launching a coordinated strike on the Dalek forward positions. The sounds of gunfire and explosions filled the air as the battle intensified.

"That's our cue," the Doctor said, turning to McKay and Sarah Jane. "Let's move."

They navigated through the corridors of Atlantis, the city now a war zone with heavily guarded areas patrolled by Daleks. The tension was palpable, every corner potentially hiding a deadly threat.

As they approached the entrance to the docking bay where the Dalek control ship was stationed, they encountered a squad of Daleks. "EX-TER-MIN-ATE!" the Daleks chanted, their weapons charging.

"Take cover!" the Doctor shouted, pulling Sarah Jane behind a column as energy beams lanced through the air.

McKay, his fingers flying over his tablet, hacked into the local defense grid. "Give me a second... there! Automated turrets activated."

The turrets sprang to life, firing at the Daleks and providing the team with a momentary reprieve. "Go, now!" McKay urged, leading the way towards the docking bay.

They sprinted through the corridor, the sound of Dalek reinforcements growing louder behind them. "We need to get to the control ship's access point," the Doctor said, his mind racing.

As they reached the docking bay, they saw the massive Dalek control ship looming before them, its hull bristling with weaponry. "There it is," Sarah Jane breathed, her eyes wide with awe and fear.

"We need to get inside and plant the disruption device," the Doctor said. "McKay, can you access their security systems?"

McKay nodded, his face set with determination. "I'm on it. Just keep me covered."

As McKay worked to disable the security protocols, the Doctor and Sarah Jane kept watch, their weapons ready. The tension was almost unbearable, every second feeling like an eternity.

"Security systems disabled," McKay announced. "We're in."

They moved quickly, entering the control ship and navigating its labyrinthine corridors. The interior was a stark contrast to the ancient beauty of Atlantis, filled with harsh metallic surfaces and the eerie hum of Dalek machinery.

"We need to get to the central control room," the Doctor said, consulting his scanner. "This way."

As they moved deeper into the ship, they encountered more Dalek patrols. "EX-TER-MIN-ATE!" the Daleks chanted, their voices echoing through the corridors.

The Doctor and Sarah Jane fired back, their shots precise and deadly. "We can't keep this up forever," Sarah Jane said, her voice strained with exertion.

"We won't have to," the Doctor replied, his eyes focused. "Just a little further."

They finally reached the central control room, a massive chamber filled with consoles and holographic displays. At the center stood a massive control node, pulsating with energy.

"That's it," McKay said, his eyes wide. "We plant the device there, and it will create a feedback loop that will disable the entire fleet."

The Doctor moved to the control node, his sonic screwdriver in hand. "Cover me. This will take a few minutes."

Sarah Jane and McKay stood guard, their weapons ready as the Doctor worked quickly, his fingers moving with practiced precision. The room was filled with the tense hum of Dalek machinery and the distant sounds of battle.

"Almost there..." the Doctor muttered, his eyes focused on the device.

Suddenly, the door to the control room burst open, and a squad of Daleks rolled in, their weapons aimed at the team. "EX-TER-MIN-ATE!" they chanted, firing their weapons.

Sarah Jane and McKay returned fire, but the Daleks were relentless. "Doctor, we need to hurry!" Sarah Jane shouted, her voice filled with urgency.

"Just a few more seconds!" the Doctor replied, his hands moving frantically.

As the Daleks closed in, McKay fired a concentrated burst, taking down two of them. "Doctor, now!"

With a final adjustment, the Doctor activated the disruption device. The control node pulsed with energy, and a wave of feedback surged through the ship. The Daleks convulsed, their systems overloaded by the feedback loop.

"WEAK-NESS... EX-PLOI-TED... SYS-TEMS FAIL-ING..." the Daleks screeched, their voices filled with panic.

"Let's get out of here!" the Doctor shouted, grabbing Sarah Jane and McKay.

They sprinted through the corridors, the ship shaking violently as the disruption spread. The sounds of Daleks malfunctioning and systems failing echoed around them.

As they reached the docking bay, the control ship's engines began to fail, and it started to collapse. They leaped into a nearby Jumper, and McKay quickly activated the controls.

"Hang on!" McKay shouted as the Jumper lifted off, escaping the collapsing ship.

They soared out of the docking bay just as the control ship exploded, a massive fireball lighting up the sky. The Dalek fleet, now leaderless and disorganized, began to retreat.

"We did it," Sarah Jane breathed, her face flushed with relief. "We actually did it."

The Doctor smiled, his eyes filled with triumph. "Yes, we did. Atlantis is safe."

As they returned to the central control room, the team erupted in cheers. The Dalek fleet was retreating, their threat neutralized.

Dr. Weir, her eyes shining with pride, addressed the team. "We faced overwhelming odds and emerged victorious. Thank you, all of you, for your bravery and determination. Atlantis stands because of you."

The Doctor, standing with Sarah Jane and McKay, felt a profound sense of accomplishment. They had faced the darkest of times and turned the tide. Atlantis was safe, and the future was theirs to protect.

As the team began to rebuild and look towards the future, the Doctor knew that their unity and resilience had been the key to their success. Together, they had overcome the impossible, and together, they would continue to defend their home.

The battle was over, but the spirit of Atlantis remained unbroken. They had faced the Dalek menace and emerged victorious, united by their courage and determination. The future was bright, and with the Doctor by their side, they were ready to face whatever challenges lay ahead.

Chapter 18: Sacrificial Heroism

The aftermath of the control ship's destruction had given the team a brief respite, but the fight was far from over. The Daleks, though weakened and disorganized, were still a threat. As the team regrouped in the central control room, they prepared for what could be their final stand.

"We've bought ourselves some time," the Doctor said, his voice steady but urgent. "But the Daleks will regroup. We need to disable their remaining ships before they can launch another assault."

Major Sheppard, his face set with determination despite his injuries, stood tall. "What's the plan, Doctor?"

The Doctor's eyes met Sheppard's, filled with a mix of admiration and concern. "We need to infiltrate their main power station. If we can disable it, we'll cripple their fleet's ability to coordinate and attack."

McKay, still working furiously at the console, added, "The power station is heavily guarded. We'll need a diversion to get inside."

Sheppard nodded, his eyes filled with resolve. "I'll lead the diversion. We'll draw their fire and give you the time you need."

Teyla, standing beside Sheppard, looked at him with concern. "John, it's too dangerous."

He placed a hand on her shoulder, his expression softening. "We don't have a choice, Teyla. This is our best shot. We need to buy the Doctor and McKay the time they need to finish this."

The Doctor, realizing the gravity of Sheppard's decision, stepped forward. "Sheppard, you don't have to do this. We can find another way."

Sheppard shook his head, his resolve unshaken. "No, Doctor. This is the only way. We've all made sacrifices, and this is mine. Just make sure you finish the job."

The team prepared for the mission, their hearts heavy with the knowledge of what lay ahead. Sheppard, Teyla, and a group of soldiers moved out to create the diversion, while the Doctor and McKay prepared to infiltrate the power station.

As they moved through the war-torn corridors, the sounds of battle grew louder. Sheppard turned to his team, his voice filled with determination. "Alright, everyone. We need to draw as many of them away as possible. Hit them hard and fast. Let's give the Doctor and McKay the time they need."

They reached a heavily guarded corridor, Daleks patrolling the area. "This is it," Sheppard said, his weapon at the ready. "On my mark... go!"

They launched their attack, energy beams and bullets filling the air. The Daleks, caught off guard, scrambled to return fire. Sheppard and his team moved with precision, taking down Daleks and drawing their attention away from the power station.

Meanwhile, the Doctor and McKay moved through a series of maintenance tunnels, using the chaos above to slip past Dalek patrols. "We're almost there," McKay said, his voice strained but focused. "Just a little further."

The Doctor nodded, his mind racing. "We need to disable their main power core. If we can overload it, it will create a chain reaction that will disable their entire fleet."

As they reached the power station, they could hear the sounds of the battle intensifying above. "Sheppard's doing his job," the Doctor said. "We need to do ours."

They entered the power station, a vast chamber filled with humming machinery and glowing conduits. McKay immediately began working on the control panels, his fingers flying over the controls.

The Doctor used his sonic screwdriver to access the core's systems. "We need to bypass the security protocols and overload the core. It's risky, but it's our best shot."

As they worked, the sounds of battle grew closer. The Daleks, realizing the diversion, began converging on the power station. "We don't have much time," McKay said, his voice filled with urgency.

Suddenly, the door to the power station burst open, and a group of Daleks rolled in. "IN-TRU-DERS WILL BE EX-TER-MIN-ATED!"

Sheppard, hearing the commotion, knew what he had to do. "Fall back!" he shouted to his team. "I'll hold them off."

Teyla, her eyes filled with anguish, grabbed his arm. "John, no!"

He looked at her, his expression filled with determination and resolve. "Go, Teyla. Protect the others. This is my fight."

With tears in her eyes, Teyla nodded and retreated with the rest of the team, leaving Sheppard to face the Daleks alone.

As the Daleks advanced, Sheppard fired relentlessly, his weapon blazing. "You want me? Come and get me!" he shouted, his voice echoing through the chamber.

The Doctor and McKay, hearing the sounds of the battle, worked frantically to finish their task. "We're almost there!" the Doctor shouted, his hands moving with blinding speed.

Sheppard continued to fight, taking down Dalek after Dalek, but he was outnumbered. A Dalek beam struck him in the side, and he fell to the ground, gasping in pain.

With his last ounce of strength, Sheppard aimed his weapon at the power core. "For Atlantis," he whispered, firing a final shot.

The energy beam struck the core, causing it to overload. The chamber was filled with a blinding light as the core began to meltdown.

"Get down!" the Doctor shouted, pulling McKay to the ground as the explosion ripped through the power station.

The shockwave surged through the Dalek fleet, disabling their systems and causing their ships to crash and burn. The threat was neutralized, but the cost had been high.

As the dust settled, the Doctor and McKay stumbled to their feet, their ears ringing from the explosion. "Sheppard," the Doctor said, his voice filled with sorrow.

They found Sheppard lying on the ground, his body battered and broken. Teyla and the rest of the team rushed in, their faces filled with grief.

Teyla knelt beside Sheppard, tears streaming down her face. "John, no..."

Sheppard looked up at her, his eyes filled with pain but also with peace. "We did it," he whispered. "Atlantis is safe."

The Doctor knelt beside him, his heart heavy. "Thank you, Sheppard. Your sacrifice saved us all."

Sheppard managed a weak smile. "Take care of them, Doctor. Make sure... make sure it was worth it."

With those final words, Major John Sheppard, the fearless leader and beloved friend, closed his eyes for the last time.

The team, their hearts shattered by the loss, stood in silent mourning. The cost of their victory had been great, but Sheppard's sacrifice had ensured their survival.

As they returned to the central control room, the weight of their loss hung heavy in the air. Dr. Weir, her eyes filled with tears, addressed the team. "John Sheppard gave his life to protect us. We honor his memory by continuing to fight, to rebuild, and to ensure that his sacrifice was not in vain."

The Doctor, standing beside her, vowed silently to himself. "I will honor your sacrifice, John. We will defeat the Daleks, and we will protect Atlantis."

The defenders of Atlantis, united by their shared grief and determination, began to rebuild. They had faced the darkest of times and emerged victorious, but the cost had been high. Yet, they knew that Sheppard's spirit would live on in their hearts and their resolve.

As they looked to the future, the team knew that they had the strength and the courage to face whatever challenges lay ahead. They would honor Sheppard's memory by continuing to defend their home and their future.

And with the Doctor by their side, they were ready to face whatever came next. The fight for Atlantis was far from over, but they were more determined than ever to ensure their victory.

Chapter 19: The Doctor's Gambit

The loss of Major Sheppard weighed heavily on the hearts of the Atlantis team, but there was no time to grieve. The Dalek threat still loomed, and the Doctor knew that their final stand was upon them. With the Dalek fleet crippled but not yet defeated, he needed to execute his final gambit to end the threat once and for all.

In the central control room, the Doctor stood before the remaining leaders of Atlantis. Dr. Weir, McKay, Teyla, and Sarah Jane gathered around him, their faces marked by exhaustion and determination.

"We've lost many good people," the Doctor began, his voice steady but filled with emotion. "But Sheppard's sacrifice has given us a chance. We need to end this now."

McKay, his eyes red from sleepless nights, nodded. "What's the plan, Doctor?"

The Doctor activated a holographic display, showing the Dalek fleet and their key positions. "The Dalek fleet is in disarray, but their command structure is still intact. We need to strike at their central command ship. If we can disable it, we can break their hold on Atlantis."

Dr. Weir's eyes narrowed. "How do we get to their command ship?"

The Doctor smiled, a glint of determination in his eyes. "We use Atlantis' technology. The city has a powerful energy weapon, designed by the Ancients. It's located in the deepest part of the city, in a hidden chamber. If we can activate it, we can target the Dalek command ship and destroy it."

Teyla stepped forward, her expression resolute. "What do you need from us?"

"We need to split into two teams," the Doctor explained. "One team will go to the hidden chamber and activate the weapon. The other team will create a diversion to draw the Daleks' attention away from the chamber."

McKay, his fingers already flying over the console, began accessing the necessary data. "I'll go with the team to activate the weapon. I know the systems inside and out."

The Doctor nodded. "Good. Sarah Jane and I will lead the diversion team. We need to draw as many Daleks as possible away from the hidden chamber."

Dr. Weir placed a hand on the Doctor's arm. "Be careful, Doctor. We've already lost so much."

The Doctor's eyes softened. "I will, Elizabeth. We all will."

The teams quickly mobilized, each member acutely aware of the importance of their mission. McKay, Teyla, and a group of engineers made their way to the hidden chamber, while the Doctor, Sarah Jane, and a squad of soldiers prepared to launch the diversion.

As they moved through the city, the tension was palpable. The sounds of distant battles echoed through the corridors, a constant reminder of the stakes.

In the hidden chamber, McKay and his team worked quickly to activate the Ancient weapon. "This system is incredibly complex," McKay muttered, his fingers flying over the controls. "But if we can get it online, it will be powerful enough to take out the Dalek command ship."

Teyla, her eyes scanning the chamber for any signs of danger, stood guard. "We will protect you, Rodney. Just focus on the task at hand."

Meanwhile, the Doctor and Sarah Jane led their team towards the Dalek's stronghold, ready to create the diversion. "We need to make as much noise as possible," the Doctor said, his eyes filled with determination. "Let's give McKay the time he needs."

They launched their attack, energy beams and bullets flying through the air. The Daleks, caught off guard, scrambled to respond. "EX-TER-MIN-ATE!" they chanted, their weapons firing back.

Sarah Jane moved with precision and skill, her energy pistol taking down Daleks with each shot. "Doctor, we need to keep them focused on us!"

The Doctor, using his sonic screwdriver, created a series of explosions that disoriented the Daleks. "Keep up the pressure! We can't let them realize our true objective."

Back in the hidden chamber, McKay finally succeeded in activating the weapon. The chamber hummed with power, and a massive energy beam began to charge. "We've done it!" McKay shouted, his face lit with triumph. "The weapon is ready to fire!"

Teyla's eyes widened. "We need to coordinate with the Doctor. The timing must be perfect."

McKay activated his comms. "Doctor, the weapon is ready. We need you to target the Dalek command ship."

The Doctor, still in the heat of battle, heard McKay's message. "Understood, Rodney. We'll handle it from here."

He turned to Sarah Jane, his eyes filled with determination. "This is it. We need to get to the highest point in the city to target the command ship. Are you ready?"

Sarah Jane nodded, her expression resolute. "Let's do it."

They made their way to the tallest tower in Atlantis, dodging Dalek patrols and using their knowledge of the city to stay ahead of the enemy. As they reached the top, they could see the Dalek command ship hovering ominously above the city.

The Doctor activated his sonic screwdriver, interfacing with the Ancient weapon. "We need to lock onto the command ship. Once we have a clear shot, we fire."

Sarah Jane stood by his side, her weapon ready. "I've got your back, Doctor."

As the weapon's targeting system locked onto the Dalek command ship, the Doctor's eyes narrowed. "Now, Rodney! Fire the weapon!"

A massive beam of energy shot from the hidden chamber, arcing through the sky and striking the Dalek command ship. The ship convulsed, its systems failing under the immense power of the Ancient weapon.

"SYS-TEMS FAIL-ING... COM-MAND STRUC-TURE COM-PROMISED..." the Dalek Supreme's voice echoed through the comms, filled with panic.

The Doctor and Sarah Jane watched as the command ship began to break apart, explosions rippling through its hull. "We did it," Sarah Jane breathed, her eyes wide with awe. "We actually did it."

But their victory was short-lived. A portion of the command ship broke off, plummeting towards the city. "We need to get out of here!" the Doctor shouted, grabbing Sarah Jane's hand and running for cover.

As the debris crashed into the city, the Doctor and Sarah Jane barely escaped the blast. The control room shook violently, and the air was filled with the sounds of destruction.

"We need to regroup with the others," the Doctor said, his voice filled with urgency.

They made their way back to the central control room, where McKay, Teyla, and the rest of the team awaited them. "The Dalek command ship is destroyed," the Doctor announced. "Their fleet is severely crippled."

Dr. Weir's eyes filled with relief and gratitude. "Thank you, Doctor. You've saved us all."

But their celebration was cut short as a squad of Daleks burst into the control room. "EX-TER-MIN-ATE!" they chanted, their weapons charging.

The Doctor, his face filled with resolve, stepped forward. "This ends now. Sarah Jane, Teyla, McKay—let's finish this."

They engaged the Daleks in a final, desperate battle. The air was filled with the sounds of energy beams and explosions as the team fought with everything they had.

The Doctor, using his knowledge of Dalek technology, created a feedback loop with his sonic screwdriver. "Sarah Jane, Teyla, cover me!"

Sarah Jane and Teyla fired relentlessly at the Daleks, their precision and skill taking down the enemy one by one. "We've got this, Doctor!" Sarah Jane shouted, her voice filled with determination.

The Doctor activated the feedback loop, sending a surge of energy through the Dalek systems. "This is for Sheppard," he whispered, his eyes filled with fury and resolve.

The Daleks convulsed, their systems overloaded by the feedback loop. "MAL-FUNC-TION... SYS-TEMS FAIL-ING..." they screeched, their voices filled with panic.

With a final, ear-splitting explosion, the Daleks were destroyed. The control room fell silent, the only sound the distant hum of the city's machinery.

The Doctor, his heart heavy with the weight of their victory, turned to the team. "It's over. Atlantis is safe."

Dr. Weir, her eyes filled with tears, stepped forward. "Thank you, Doctor. We couldn't have done it without you."

The Doctor shook his head, his expression filled with humility. "We did this together. Atlantis stands because of all of us."

As the team began to assess the damage and tend to the wounded, the Doctor and Sarah Jane stood together, their hearts filled with a mix of triumph and sorrow.

"We did it, Doctor," Sarah Jane said, her voice filled with quiet pride.

The Doctor nodded, his eyes filled with determination. "Yes, but the cost was high. We must honor those we've lost by ensuring that Atlantis remains a beacon of hope and resilience."

As the first light of dawn broke over the city, the defenders of Atlantis knew that they had faced the darkness and emerged victorious. The future was theirs to shape, and they would do so with the same unwavering resolve that had seen them through the darkest of times.

With the Dalek threat finally defeated, Atlantis stood strong and proud, a testament to the courage and determination of its people. And with the Doctor by their side, they were ready to face whatever challenges lay ahead, united by their shared purpose and unbreakable bond.

Chapter 20: Victory at a Cost

The final echoes of battle faded, leaving Atlantis in an uneasy silence. The city, though battered and scarred, remained standing. The defenders, weary but resolute, began the arduous task of driving out the last remnants of the Dalek forces.

In the central control room, Dr. Weir coordinated the efforts. "We need to sweep the entire city, ensuring there are no remaining Daleks. Leave no stone unturned."

Teyla, her face a mask of determination, nodded. "I will lead the search teams. We cannot afford to leave any Dalek behind."

Sarah Jane, standing beside the Doctor, looked at the holographic map of Atlantis. "We've come so far, Doctor. This city, these people—they've been through so much."

The Doctor, his eyes reflecting the weight of their journey, nodded. "Yes, Sarah Jane. But they're strong. Atlantis will endure."

As Teyla and her teams spread out across the city, systematically clearing each sector of Dalek presence, the atmosphere remained tense. The threat had been neutralized, but the scars of battle were fresh and painful.

Hours passed, and gradually, the reports came in—sector after sector declared clear. The remaining Daleks were either destroyed or had fled. The city was secure.

In the central control room, a quiet sense of relief began to settle. Dr. Weir addressed her team, her voice carrying the weight of their shared struggle. "We have regained control of our city. The Dalek threat has been eliminated. This victory belongs to each and every one of you. Thank you."

A subdued cheer rose from the assembled personnel, their faces showing a mixture of relief and sorrow. The cost of their victory was high, and the losses weighed heavily on their hearts.

Dr. Weir turned to the Doctor, her eyes filled with gratitude. "Doctor, I cannot thank you enough. Your knowledge, your courage—they were instrumental in saving Atlantis. We owe you our lives."

The Doctor shook his head, his expression humble. "Elizabeth, you and your team fought bravely. This victory is a testament to your resilience and unity. I was just one part of it."

Sarah Jane stepped forward, her eyes filled with emotion. "Doctor, you always find a way to bring out the best in people. You've done it again here."

The Doctor smiled, a touch of sadness in his eyes. "I only helped them see what they were capable of. The real strength lies within them."

As the team began to reflect on their journey, Teyla returned to the control room, her face a mixture of triumph and sorrow. "The city is clear. We have driven the Daleks out."

Dr. Weir nodded, her expression somber. "Thank you, Teyla. Now we can begin to rebuild."

The atmosphere in the control room shifted to one of quiet reflection. The defenders of Atlantis, though victorious, were acutely aware of the sacrifices that had been made. The faces of the fallen haunted their thoughts, their absence a poignant reminder of the cost of their struggle.

A memorial service was held in the central plaza, a solemn gathering to honor those who had given their lives. Dr. Weir stood before the assembled personnel, her voice steady but filled with emotion.

"Today, we honor our fallen comrades. They fought with bravery and determination, giving their lives to protect Atlantis. We will remember them, and we will carry their legacy forward."

Sheppard's absence was felt keenly, his sacrifice a poignant reminder of the cost of their victory. Teyla, standing beside his memorial, whispered a silent prayer, her heart heavy with grief.

As the service concluded, the team dispersed, each person finding their own way to cope with the loss. The Doctor and Sarah Jane stood together, reflecting on the journey they had shared.

"Doctor, what happens now?" Sarah Jane asked, her voice soft.

The Doctor looked out over the city, a sense of calm settling over him. "Now, they rebuild. Atlantis has faced incredible challenges, but they will rise stronger. And we—well, we have more adventures ahead."

Dr. Weir approached them, her expression one of gratitude and determination. "Doctor, Sarah Jane, you will always have a place here in Atlantis. Your contributions were invaluable, and you are part of our family now."

The Doctor nodded, his eyes warm. "Thank you, Elizabeth. It's been an honor to fight alongside you."

As the Doctor and Sarah Jane prepared to leave, the team gathered to bid them farewell. McKay, his usual sarcasm tempered by genuine respect, extended his hand. "Doctor, you're not so bad for a time-traveling alien."

The Doctor shook his hand, a smile playing at his lips. "And you, Rodney, are one of the finest minds I've ever had the pleasure of working with. Take care of this city."

Teyla, her eyes filled with gratitude, stepped forward. "Thank you, Doctor. You've shown us what we're capable of. We will honor your teachings."

Sarah Jane embraced Teyla, her voice choked with emotion. "Stay strong, Teyla. You're a warrior and a leader."

As the Doctor and Sarah Jane made their way to the TARDIS, the team watched with a mixture of sadness and hope. The blue box, a symbol of endless possibilities, stood ready to whisk them away to new adventures.

Dr. Weir, her heart filled with a renewed sense of purpose, addressed her team one last time. "We have faced the darkness and emerged into the light. Atlantis stands because of our unity and strength. We will rebuild, and we will honor the memory of those we've lost."

The TARDIS doors closed, and with a familiar whirring sound, it disappeared, leaving behind a team forever changed by their journey.

The defenders of Atlantis looked to the future, their hearts heavy with loss but filled with hope.

The battle had been won, and though the cost was high, they knew that they had the strength to rebuild and protect their home. The Doctor's legacy would live on in their hearts, guiding them as they faced whatever challenges lay ahead.

And so, Atlantis stood as a beacon of resilience and unity, a testament to the courage and determination of its people. The future was theirs to shape, and they would do so with unwavering resolve, honoring the sacrifices that had been made and embracing the hope that lay ahead.

Chapter 21: Aftermath and Recovery

The sun rose over the horizon, casting a golden glow on the battered yet resilient city of Atlantis. The scars of the Dalek invasion were evident everywhere, from the damaged buildings to the wounded personnel, but the spirit of Atlantis was unbroken. The process of rebuilding and recovery had begun.

The central control room buzzed with activity as the team coordinated efforts to repair the city and assess the damage. Dr. Weir, her face marked with exhaustion but also determination, stood at the center, directing operations.

"We need to prioritize critical systems—power, water, and medical facilities," she instructed, her voice calm and authoritative. "McKay, I want a full assessment of our infrastructure. We need to know what we're dealing with."

McKay, his usual bravado tempered by the recent events, nodded. "I'm on it, Elizabeth. I'll get my team working on it right away."

The Doctor, standing beside McKay, offered his assistance. "Rodney, if you'd like, I can help with the repairs. My sonic screwdriver can speed up the process."

McKay, who had often clashed with the Doctor's unconventional methods, looked at him with newfound respect. "I'd appreciate that, Doctor. We could use all the help we can get."

As they set to work, the Doctor used his sonic screwdriver to repair damaged circuits and systems, while McKay and his team focused on restoring the main power grid. The two worked side by side, their previous disagreements set aside in the face of their shared goal.

Sarah Jane, meanwhile, helped organize the medical teams, ensuring that the wounded received the care they needed. She moved through the medical bay, offering words of encouragement and support to those who had fought so bravely.

"You're doing great," she said to a young soldier, his arm in a sling. "We'll get through this together."

Teyla, leading a group of volunteers, oversaw the distribution of supplies and the rebuilding of damaged structures. Her presence was a source of strength and inspiration to those around her.

"Every contribution counts," she said, her voice firm but kind. "We rebuild our home together."

As the day wore on, the Doctor and McKay made significant progress in restoring the city's systems. They paused for a moment, taking a break from their work.

"Doctor," McKay began, his voice uncharacteristically soft, "I wanted to say thank you. For everything. I know I haven't always been the easiest to work with, but... you've shown me a lot."

The Doctor smiled, his eyes warm. "Rodney, you've done incredible work here. Atlantis is lucky to have you. And I'm glad we could work together. We make a pretty good team, don't you think?"

McKay chuckled, a genuine smile spreading across his face. "Yeah, I guess we do."

Dr. Weir approached them, her expression one of gratitude. "Doctor, McKay, the progress you've made is remarkable. Thank you. We couldn't have done this without you."

The Doctor shook his head. "This was a team effort, Elizabeth. Everyone played a crucial role. Atlantis is strong because of the people who live here."

As they continued their work, the sense of unity and purpose grew stronger. The defenders of Atlantis, though exhausted and grieving their losses, were determined to rebuild and protect their home.

In the following days, the city slowly began to return to a semblance of normalcy. The power grid was restored, and essential services were brought back online. The wounded received the care they needed, and the process of rebuilding continued with renewed vigor.

The Doctor, ever the wanderer, knew that his time in Atlantis was coming to an end. He approached Dr. Weir, McKay, and Teyla, his eyes filled with a mixture of pride and sorrow.

"Elizabeth, Rodney, Teyla," he began, "I've stayed longer than I usually do, but it's time for me to move on. There are other places that need help, and other adventures waiting."

Dr. Weir nodded, her eyes glistening with unshed tears. "We will miss you, Doctor. You've become a part of our family here. Thank you for everything."

McKay, his usual sarcasm replaced with genuine respect, extended his hand. "Doctor, you've been a real pain sometimes, but I wouldn't have it any other way. Thank you."

The Doctor shook McKay's hand, a smile playing at his lips. "Take care of this city, Rodney. You're one of the finest minds I've ever met."

Teyla stepped forward, her eyes filled with gratitude. "Thank you, Doctor. For showing us our strength and for standing with us."

Sarah Jane, standing beside the Doctor, looked at him with a mix of admiration and affection. "Ready for the next adventure, Doctor?"

The Doctor nodded, his eyes twinkling. "Always, Sarah Jane. Always."

As they made their way to the TARDIS, the team gathered to bid them farewell. The blue box, a symbol of endless possibilities, stood ready to whisk them away to new adventures.

Dr. Weir addressed the assembled personnel, her voice strong and steady. "Today, we say goodbye to our friends, the Doctor and Sarah Jane. They have shown us what we are capable of and have stood with us in our darkest hour. We honor them and the sacrifices made by so many. Atlantis will endure because of their bravery and our unwavering resolve."

A cheer rose from the crowd, their faces reflecting a mixture of hope and sorrow. The Doctor and Sarah Jane waved goodbye as the TARDIS doors closed. With a familiar whirring sound, the TARDIS disappeared, leaving behind a team forever changed by their journey.

The defenders of Atlantis looked to the future with renewed determination. They had faced the darkest of times and emerged stronger.

The Doctor's legacy would live on in their hearts, guiding them as they continued to rebuild and protect their home.

Atlantis stood as a beacon of resilience and unity, a testament to the courage and determination of its people. The future was bright, and with the lessons learned and the bonds forged in the fires of battle, they were ready to face whatever challenges lay ahead.

And so, the city of Atlantis began to heal and rebuild, its spirit unbroken and its people united by their shared purpose and unwavering resolve. The Doctor had shown them their strength, and they would carry that strength forward, honoring the sacrifices made and embracing the hope that lay ahead.

Chapter 22: Farewell to Friends

The morning sun cast a warm glow over the city of Atlantis, reflecting off the tranquil waters and illuminating the buildings that had withstood the storm of the Dalek invasion. The air was filled with a sense of renewal and hope, tempered by the bittersweet knowledge that it was time for the Doctor and Sarah Jane to bid farewell to their newfound friends.

In the central plaza, the Atlantis team gathered to see them off. The TARDIS stood nearby, its familiar blue presence a stark contrast to the futuristic architecture of the city. The Doctor and Sarah Jane stood together, taking in the scene, their hearts heavy with the impending goodbyes.

Dr. Weir stepped forward, her eyes filled with gratitude. "Doctor, Sarah Jane, I can't begin to express how much you've done for us. Your courage and knowledge saved Atlantis. Thank you."

The Doctor smiled warmly. "Elizabeth, it's been an honor. You and your team have shown incredible bravery and resilience. Atlantis is strong because of you."

Dr. Weir reached into her pocket and pulled out a small, intricately crafted pendant. "This is a token of our gratitude. It's made from a rare mineral found only in the Pegasus galaxy. It symbolizes strength and unity. Please, take it as a reminder of our alliance and friendship."

The Doctor accepted the pendant, his eyes reflecting his deep appreciation. "Thank you, Elizabeth. I will treasure this always."

Next, Teyla approached, her expression a mix of sadness and respect. "Doctor, you've shown us what we're capable of. Thank you for your guidance and for standing with us."

The Doctor opened his arms, and Teyla embraced him warmly. "Take care, Teyla. You're a remarkable leader and a fierce warrior."

Sarah Jane received a hug from Teyla as well. "Stay strong, Teyla. You've been an inspiration."

McKay stepped forward, his usual sarcasm giving way to a rare moment of genuine emotion. "Doctor, you've been a real pain sometimes, but I have to admit, we couldn't have done it without you."

The Doctor laughed, embracing McKay. "Rodney, you've done amazing work here. Keep pushing the boundaries of what's possible."

As they pulled away, McKay glanced at the TARDIS and smirked. "I still can't believe that thing actually works. It looks like it was put together by a child with a paint set."

The Doctor chuckled. "She may not look like much, but she's got it where it counts."

Dr. Beckett approached next, his face lined with weariness but also relief. "Doctor, thank you for everything. You've saved so many lives."

The Doctor hugged Beckett, feeling the weight of the struggles they had shared. "You're a brilliant doctor, Carson. Keep taking care of these people."

Sarah Jane received a warm hug from Beckett as well. "You've been wonderful, Sarah Jane. Thank you."

Major Lorne, his uniform bearing the marks of battle, stepped forward. "Doctor, it's been an honor. We'll never forget what you've done for us."

The Doctor embraced Lorne, appreciating the soldier's steadfast loyalty. "Stay strong, Major. Atlantis is in good hands with you."

Finally, Dr. Weir approached once more, her eyes misty with emotion. "Doctor, Sarah Jane, you will always have a place here in Atlantis. Our doors are open to you, anytime."

The Doctor and Sarah Jane embraced her warmly. "Thank you, Elizabeth. We'll always remember our time here," the Doctor said.

As the goodbyes concluded, the Doctor and Sarah Jane turned to face the TARDIS. The Doctor paused, looking back at the team one last time. "Take care of each other. Atlantis is a beacon of hope and strength. Never forget that."

Sarah Jane smiled warmly at their friends. "Thank you all. We'll miss you."

With a final wave, the Doctor and Sarah Jane entered the TARDIS. The familiar hum of the time machine filled the air, and moments later, it disappeared with a whooshing sound, leaving the team standing in the plaza, their hearts full of gratitude and resolve.

Dr. Weir turned to her team, her voice strong and steady. "We've faced incredible challenges, but we've emerged stronger. Let's honor the Doctor and Sarah Jane by continuing to build a better future for Atlantis."

McKay, his usual skepticism replaced by genuine admiration, added, "And let's remember that even in the darkest times, there's always hope. We've seen that firsthand."

Teyla nodded, her eyes filled with determination. "We are united, and we are strong. Atlantis will endure."

As the team dispersed to continue their work, the sense of unity and purpose was palpable. They had faced the Dalek menace and emerged victorious, their bonds forged in the fires of battle.

Atlantis stood as a testament to their courage and resilience, a beacon of hope in a galaxy filled with uncertainty. The Doctor's legacy would live on in their hearts, guiding them as they faced whatever challenges lay ahead.

And so, with the dawn of a new day, the defenders of Atlantis looked to the future with unwavering resolve, ready to protect their home and embrace the hope that lay ahead. The journey had been long and arduous, but they had proven that together, they could overcome any obstacle and build a brighter future for all.

Chapter 23: Reflections and Departures

The familiar hum of the TARDIS enveloped the Doctor and Sarah Jane as they stood in the control room, the lights and sounds of the ancient time machine providing a comforting backdrop. The adventure in Atlantis had been one of their most challenging and rewarding experiences, and now, as they prepared to depart, they took a moment to reflect on what they had accomplished.

Sarah Jane leaned against the console, her eyes filled with a mix of exhaustion and satisfaction. "Doctor, Atlantis... it was incredible. Terrifying, but incredible. I can't believe everything we went through."

The Doctor nodded, his expression thoughtful. "Yes, it was quite the adventure, wasn't it? The people of Atlantis are remarkable. Their resilience, their unity... it's inspiring."

Sarah Jane smiled warmly. "They were so brave. And you, Doctor, you showed them what they were capable of. You always do."

The Doctor's eyes softened. "I only helped them see their own strength, Sarah Jane. They did the rest. They've shown that even in the face of impossible odds, hope and determination can prevail."

She walked around the console, her fingers trailing over the various controls. "What do you think will happen to them now?"

The Doctor leaned back, his eyes gazing into the distance as if he could still see the city of Atlantis. "They'll rebuild, stronger than ever. They'll honor the sacrifices made and continue to protect their home. Atlantis will endure, and they'll forge a future filled with hope and possibility."

Sarah Jane nodded, her heart swelling with pride for their friends. "It's amazing how much of an impact you have on people, Doctor. You change lives."

The Doctor smiled, a touch of sadness in his eyes. "And they change mine, Sarah Jane. Every place we visit, every person we meet—they all leave their mark. Atlantis will always hold a special place in my hearts."

They stood in companionable silence for a moment, each lost in their thoughts. The TARDIS, ever patient, waited for its next journey.

Finally, the Doctor moved to the console, his fingers dancing over the controls. "Well, Sarah Jane, where to next? The universe is vast, and there are endless adventures waiting for us."

Sarah Jane's eyes sparkled with excitement. "Anywhere but here. Somewhere new, somewhere we can make a difference."

The Doctor grinned, his enthusiasm infectious. "Excellent! Let's see where the TARDIS takes us."

He pulled a lever, and the TARDIS began to dematerialize from Atlantis, the familiar whooshing sound filling the control room. As they left the city behind, the Doctor and Sarah Jane felt a mixture of anticipation and nostalgia.

The journey through the time vortex was smooth, the TARDIS guiding them to their next destination. The Doctor, his eyes fixed on the monitor, contemplated their next adventure. "I wonder where we'll end up. A distant galaxy? A forgotten corner of history? The possibilities are endless."

Sarah Jane stood beside him, her excitement palpable. "Wherever it is, Doctor, I know it will be extraordinary."

The Doctor smiled, his eyes twinkling with the promise of new discoveries. "Indeed, Sarah Jane. Indeed."

As the TARDIS continued its journey, the Doctor reflected on their time in Atlantis. The bonds they had formed, the lives they had touched, and the lessons they had learned would stay with them forever. It was a reminder of why they traveled—to explore, to protect, and to inspire.

The TARDIS's engines hummed softly, and the Doctor glanced at Sarah Jane, his heart filled with gratitude for her companionship. "You know, Sarah Jane, I'm glad you're here. This journey wouldn't be the same without you."

Sarah Jane smiled warmly. "I wouldn't want to be anywhere else, Doctor. Here's to the next adventure."

The Doctor raised an imaginary glass, his eyes bright with anticipation. "To the next adventure."

And so, as the TARDIS hurtled through time and space, the Doctor and Sarah Jane looked forward to whatever lay ahead. The universe was vast and filled with wonders, and they were ready to face it together.

The adventures of the Doctor and Sarah Jane would continue, their spirits undaunted and their hearts open to the endless possibilities that awaited them. With the TARDIS as their guide, they would explore the farthest reaches of the cosmos, always seeking to make a difference, to protect, and to inspire.

As they embarked on their next journey, the Doctor's thoughts lingered on Atlantis and the friends they had made there. The city would continue to thrive, a beacon of hope and resilience, just as the Doctor and Sarah Jane would continue their travels, bringing light to the darkest corners of the universe.

And so, with a final glance at the swirling vortex outside the TARDIS doors, the Doctor smiled, ready for whatever came next. The adventure was far from over, and with Sarah Jane by his side, he knew they could face anything.

The TARDIS hummed with life, and the Doctor's hearts swelled with the promise of new beginnings. "Allons-y, Sarah Jane. Let's see what's out there."

With a shared look of excitement and determination, the Doctor and Sarah Jane set off into the unknown, their journey continuing, their spirits undaunted, and their hearts filled with the thrill of adventure. The universe awaited, and they were ready.

Chapter 24: A New Beginning

Atlantis was no longer the city under siege; it was a city reborn. The sun rose over the horizon, casting a golden glow on the rebuilt structures, the scars of the battle slowly healing. The people of Atlantis, though weary and marked by their losses, stood united and resilient, ready to face the future.

In the central control room, Dr. Weir addressed her team, her voice filled with both solemnity and hope. "We have faced the unthinkable and emerged stronger. We honor those we have lost by continuing to build a better future for Atlantis."

The room was filled with nods of agreement and determined expressions. McKay, his usual bravado tempered by the experiences they had shared, stood beside Teyla and Major Lorne.

"We need to ensure our defenses are stronger than ever," McKay said, his voice resolute. "No more surprises. We'll be ready for anything."

Teyla nodded, her gaze steady. "And we will continue to strengthen our bonds with our allies. Unity is our greatest strength."

Major Lorne, his uniform bearing the marks of battle but his spirit unbroken, added, "And we'll rebuild our city, honoring the bravery of those who fought to protect it."

Dr. Weir smiled, a mix of pride and determination in her eyes. "Then let's get to work. We have a lot to do, and I know we can accomplish anything together."

As the team dispersed to their tasks, the atmosphere in Atlantis was one of renewed purpose. Engineers and scientists worked side by side to restore and improve the city's systems. Soldiers and civilians collaborated to fortify defenses and rebuild damaged structures. The spirit of Atlantis was unyielding, a beacon of hope and resilience.

In the medical bay, Dr. Beckett moved among the patients, his heart filled with a mix of relief and sorrow. The wounded were healing, and the fallen were honored, their sacrifices never to be forgotten.

Meanwhile, in the heart of the city, the Doctor and Sarah Jane stood by the TARDIS, preparing for their departure. The time they had spent in Atlantis had left a lasting impression on them both.

"Doctor, do you think they'll be alright?" Sarah Jane asked, her eyes reflecting both concern and hope.

The Doctor nodded, his expression thoughtful. "Yes, Sarah Jane. They've shown incredible strength and unity. Atlantis will thrive. They have everything they need to face the future."

As they prepared to enter the TARDIS, Dr. Weir, McKay, Teyla, and Major Lorne approached for one final goodbye.

"Doctor, Sarah Jane," Dr. Weir began, her voice filled with gratitude, "thank you. You've shown us what we're capable of and have given us hope. We will never forget you."

The Doctor smiled warmly, embracing her. "It's been an honor, Elizabeth. Take care of this remarkable city."

McKay, his usual sarcasm giving way to genuine emotion, extended his hand. "Doctor, you've been... not as annoying as I thought you'd be. Thank you."

The Doctor shook McKay's hand, laughing. "High praise indeed, Rodney. Keep pushing the boundaries of what's possible."

Teyla, her eyes filled with respect, hugged the Doctor. "Thank you for standing with us. We will honor your teachings."

Major Lorne, his face reflecting his admiration, saluted the Doctor. "Safe travels, Doctor. And thank you."

Sarah Jane hugged each of them in turn, her heart heavy with the impending farewell. "You're all incredible. Keep being the heroes you are."

As the Doctor and Sarah Jane entered the TARDIS, the Atlantis team stepped back, watching with a mix of sadness and hope. The TARDIS doors closed, and with a familiar whooshing sound, it began to dematerialize.

The team stood in silence for a moment, reflecting on the journey they had shared. Then, with renewed determination, they turned back to their tasks, ready to build the future of Atlantis.

Inside the TARDIS, the Doctor and Sarah Jane stood by the console, their hearts filled with anticipation for what lay ahead. "Where to next, Doctor?" Sarah Jane asked, her eyes sparkling with excitement.

The Doctor grinned, his eyes twinkling with the thrill of new adventures. "Anywhere and everywhere, Sarah Jane. The universe is vast, and there's so much to explore."

He pulled a lever, and the TARDIS hummed with life, its engines propelling them through time and space. The familiar swirl of the time vortex enveloped them, and the Doctor's hearts swelled with the promise of new discoveries.

As they traveled, the Doctor and Sarah Jane reflected on their time in Atlantis. The bonds they had formed, the lives they had touched, and the lessons they had learned would stay with them forever. It was a reminder of why they traveled—to explore, to protect, and to inspire.

The TARDIS's journey was smooth, the destination unknown but filled with potential. The Doctor glanced at the monitor, his mind racing with possibilities. "I wonder where we'll end up next. A distant galaxy? A forgotten corner of history? The possibilities are endless."

Sarah Jane smiled, her excitement palpable. "Wherever it is, Doctor, I know it will be extraordinary."

The Doctor raised an imaginary glass, his eyes bright with anticipation. "To the next adventure."

And so, as the TARDIS hurtled through time and space, the Doctor and Sarah Jane looked forward to whatever lay ahead. The universe was vast and filled with wonders, and they were ready to face it together.

The adventures of the Doctor and Sarah Jane would continue, their spirits undaunted and their hearts open to the endless possibilities that awaited them. With the TARDIS as their guide, they would explore the farthest reaches of the cosmos, always seeking to make a difference, to protect, and to inspire.

As they embarked on their next journey, the Doctor's thoughts lingered on Atlantis and the friends they had made there. The city would continue to thrive, a beacon of hope and resilience, just as the

Doctor and Sarah Jane would continue their travels, bringing light to the darkest corners of the universe.

And so, with a final glance at the swirling vortex outside the TARDIS doors, the Doctor smiled, ready for whatever came next. The adventure was far from over, and with Sarah Jane by his side, he knew they could face anything.

The TARDIS hummed with life, and the Doctor's hearts swelled with the promise of new beginnings. "Allons-y, Sarah Jane. Let's see what's out there."

With a shared look of excitement and determination, the Doctor and Sarah Jane set off into the unknown, their journey continuing, their spirits undaunted, and their hearts filled with the thrill of adventure. The universe awaited, and they were ready.

-

-

-

<u>Message from the Author:</u>

I hope you enjoyed this book, I love astrology and knew there was not a book such as this out on the shelf. I love metaphysical items as well. Please check out my other books:

-Life of Government Benefits

-My life of Hell

-My life with Hydrocephalus

-Red Sky

-World Domination:Woman's rule

-World Domination:Woman's Rule 2: The War

-Life and Banishment of Apophis: book 1

-The Kidney Friendly Diet

-The Ultimate Hemp Cookbook

-Creating a Dispensary(legally)

-Cleanliness throughout life: the importance of showering from childhood to adulthood.

-Strong Roots: The Risks of Overcoddling children

-Hemp Horoscopes: Cosmic Insights and Earthly Healing

- Celestial Hemp Navigating the Zodiac: Through the Green Cosmos

-Astrological Hemp: Aligning The Stars with Earth's Ancient Herb

-The Astrological Guide to Hemp: Stars, Signs, and Sacred Leaves

-Green Growth: Innovative Marketing Strategies for your Hemp Products and Dispensary

-Cosmic Cannabis

-Astrological Munchies

-Henry The Hemp

-Zodiacal Roots: The Astrological Soul Of Hemp

- **Green Constellations: Intersection of Hemp and Zodiac**

-Hemp in The Houses: An astrological Adventure Through The Cannabis Galaxy

-Galactic Ganja Guide

Heavenly Hemp

Zodiac Leaves

Doctor Who Astrology

Cannastrology

Stellar Satvias and Cosmic Indicas

<u>Celestial Cannabis: A Zodiac Journey</u>

AstroHerbology: The Sky and The Soil: Volume 1

AstroHerbology:Celestial Cannabis:Volume 2

Cosmic Cannabis Cultivation

The Starry Guide to Herbal Harmony: Volume 1

The Starry Guide to Herbal Harmony: Cannabis Universe: Volume 2

Yugioh Astrology: Astrological Guide to Deck, Duels and more

Nightmare Mansion: Echoes of The Abyss

Nightmare Mansion 2: Legacy of Shadows

Nightmare Mansion 3: Shadows of the Forgotten

Nightmare Mansion 4: Echoes of the Damned

The Life and Banishment of Apophis: Book 2

Nightmare Mansion: Halls of Despair

<u>Healing with Herb: Cannabis and Hydrocephalus</u>

<u>Planetary Pot: Aligning with Astrological Herbs: Volume 1</u>

Fast Track to Freedom: 30 Days to Financial Independence Using AI, Assets, and Agile Hustles

<u>Cosmic Hemp Pathways</u>

How to Become Financially Free in 30 Days: 10,000 Paths to Prosperity

Zodiacal Herbage: Astrological Insights: Volume 1

Nightmare Mansion: Whispers in the Walls

Check out my Virtual dispensary for all your hemp needs: https://shift.store/sg1fan23477/retail

If you want solar for your home go here: https://www.harboursolar.live/apophisenterprises/

Instagrams:

@apophis_enterprises,

@hempkingdom2024,

@apophisbookemporium,

@apophisfashion,

@apophisscardshop

Twitter: @apophisenterpr1,

Tiktok:@apophisenterprise

Youtube: @sg1fan23477

Podcast:Apophis Chat Zone: https://open.spotify.com/show/5zXbrCLEV2xzCp8ybrfHsk?si=fb4d4fdbdce44dec

Newsletter: https://apophiss-newsletter-27c897.beehiiv.com/